Blood,
Dreams &
Tears

Blood, Dreams & Tears

Tim Eagle

Lake Leviathan Books

An Angry Trout Production:
Published by Lake Leviathan Books

 REGISTERED TRADEMARK

Cover Art by: Gordon Whitney

First Edition

PUBLISHER'S NOTE

This is a work of fiction. All the characters and events portrayed in this book are fictional, and any resemblance to real people or incidents is purely coincidental, but sometimes necessary because fiction often represents a part of life that everyone ignores.

To my wife, Maria, my parents, Ed & Lorraine, and my Grandmother, Ruby Jeffery; it is always their love and devotion to life, marriage, family and friends that inspire me endlessly. I love you all very much.

Contents

Life in a Sheltered Mind

The history of Stevats' is marked by a peculiar ceremony. The rituals, hosted by an elusive group of people, give a bizarre afterward to death—taboo speeches written and read about the dead, presented by a person who was exclusively invited to read or write the afterward. These customs are called Stencil Ceremonies, an outline of the deceased, unenlightened, and catering to the dark side of their lives. The people who wrote these words often used pseudonyms to shroud the fact that the dead were being disrespected. These were rare written letters that were read with masks of concealment; the readings often taking place in obscure, secretive locations.

This particular Stencil was edited afterward by an unknown author, circa 1812, found on Sunflower Street in the basement of an old house, before it was torn down in 2012.

I stood there, in front of people, people who have read their Stencil, either before me, or waiting their turn. The mask made my skin hot underneath. Its elongated nose and slanted eyes, too hard to see through, were absurd, but so was everything else in life when gazed upon for too long.

People say hate is a very nasty form of energy that takes a lot from a person, and that it's a burdensome emotion to hold onto. I couldn't agree more. My nerves inside are stone right now; I'm waiting in what the other readers called *the pulpit*, a place of proverbial purgatory before finally reading the truth about a lost loved one, and I can't believe I accepted the invitation. The place dark, obscuring the others around me and the elders running the ceremony have instructed all of us to remain silent and keep our identities unknown.

What's life if you don't take risks and tell the world

the truth? It's no different than whispering into a family pet's ears; it's no different than yelling it to *GOD* in the solitude of your own room, closet or happy place. So I've come here to this place.

It's a vast chamber, an unfamiliar plush theater that I'd never seen before. I've lived in Stevats forever; it's the very city I've been part of my whole life, my own prison at times, and never saw such ornate beauty bestowed before me. It's large, dark wood carvings of gothic proportion, and the dim yellow lighting spoke of age. It was beautifully crafted really, almost too beautiful for what I'm about to propose before a bunch of strangers in the audience or the people in front, reading, or behind, rattling their pages in anticipation. I debated many nights to reading my own after the invite; I always believed that after your father passed away that I'd be a better person.

I convinced myself that I would start going to mass more frequently, become a more devout Christian in the shitty world my life had become. I was going to give more, save less. I was going to listen more, speak less. Care more and stop being so selfish. But this story, the story I'm about to read is reason enough to resist those changes. It's negative, darkly fascinating to everyone but me, the sole bearer. It's the lifetime achievement of nothing because I've let the premise burn inside like the evil incarnate it is. This is the only way to carve the energy out, to dig deep within and throw it out to a world, as if feeding lions at the zoo, and get rid of it once and for all.

People must wake! I must be awake for it!

It's close to my turn, and my stomach knots up. My

bowels are churning, and the nerves inside are like no other. It's a course of adrenaline, and fear, excitement, and dull repetition, an incessant repetition that has beat itself inside me, but if I don't do this, I will be nothing, I will not move forward in life, and I will never lift my head again, will always look to the ground, my aspirations in life stamped out because I didn't take this chance. Time to walk, the stairs to the podium are clear, and the last reader finished a Stencil written of her son. It's my turn now. I hope this works.

A staring race of masked faces is enamored by each reader, they await me. I am no exception. I stand staring through the ridiculous mask that they made me wear. The mask will be tossed on a blazing fire that's on stage next to the podium if I choose to run off and take it off. If I want to stay I'll stay, it's my choice, life is but a grand coffin of choices and I don't fear any of them like I might have while you were with me.

The heat radiates and warms; the sweat beneath the mask is thick, down my face, mixed with tears. My eyes pool as I take a deep breath, and wallow once again over the gaping masses ready to hear my Stencil. I will never repeat these words again, and hope to never feel this pain, this hatred, as much as I do at this moment. I will read, my head high, because it's the only thing I have in life left to do. Maybe afterward it will all vanish like some act of smoke and mirrors, I can only hope for that blessing.

*

You were young, yes, a happy little girl. Our shinning diamond, really. Your father and I watched your tiny hands play, your mind always a whirlwind of ideas. The smile on your face beamed. We looked at you, our flesh and blood, and our biological little person, made up of our love. You made us happy, you played hard, you worked hard, you were always willing to please, to do great things, and always set out for those great things. But all of that came to a halt. To think I blamed myself for your demons. Hindsight, it looks bitter and dark, but its right, it's always right.

You kept to yourself most times. We had to be mind-readers, your dad and me, just to know what you needed or wanted. It was always a guessing game for us. You rejected your father's words and touch; it hurt me to see this. He would reach for your hand and you would pull it away as if it burned you. He would try to kiss you good night, and you would scream. I thought it was him, thought that maybe he touched you, GOD rest his soul, inappropriately, but he was never alone with you, you never allowed it. You rejected him, and your father was the kindest, most giving man in the world, who would have, despite the rude coldness you gave him, bent over backwards for you.

You disregarded any kind of motherly advice I had to share with you, before it was the time in your life that would justify that sort of behavior. You rejected me with a cold snub, horrible words like, "bitch", "whore", "basket case", or "fucker." It hurt, and words, they can't be erased. They hang in an ethereal world on another frequency and often echo back in my head. They sting, nonetheless, and they are bitter, but I've learned to embrace them, and be just what you called me, I was prepared to reciprocate.

You sunk into a world that your father and I gasped

at. It didn't include morality, didn't include the hard work ethics that we ever taught you. It did include a fallen sickness with laziness, with utter disregard for anything ever taught to you, and you had become, and I used to struggle saying this up until now, an asshole.

I woke to the idea that your life was a downward spiral plunging into the abyss. I found the truth behind it. I found the fur pelts you took from animals in your closet. You acted out because you were warning me. You wanted me as your prey, but I wasn't going to have it. I had already become that part for you when you insulted me. The way you spoke to me. I was so ready for you to try and take something other than my mind, believe me. The knife still lies next to the revolver under my bed, waiting for your attempt.

Victim is a word I don't use loosely; it's a word that best describes you because you've been one your whole life. You blamed the world for your flaws, or your father and I. You pointed your finger at everyone around you, school mates, teachers, and any other authority figure who ever tried to hold you accountable, shame on you. These were signs that were waved in front of my face like blatant battle flags, yet ignorance served me. The charming small town mentality, that isn't so charming when you have to face it head on, kept me in its soothing arms, like the comforts of horse blinders. Your trophies of pelts, the trinkets I stumbled on, and my Christian beliefs, although they had slowly vanquished, slowly dissipated with each new path I was forced upon, tipped me over the edge.

I don't know how I survived, but the struggle to get through to you, to point you in the right direction without you blowing up, was a challenge I was going to face. Your father's health put a halt to that. I will always blame you for his deterioration, because you sucked energy out of our house, out of our very souls, until his feeble energy was consumed. He was horrified, terrified, and crawled so far inside himself, I couldn't reach him anymore. Until finally, with his milky white gaze and his mouth open, he died and literally fell from our couch, in front of me, onto the hard floor, never to wake again.

I woke up just to see it!

I wept, my mind was frayed an endless stream of death to the horror I witnessed.

You were the bride to that black shawl that shrouded you. For how long, I'm not sure. As I speak, I'm getting angrier at you! You were my child and as I don't like admitting it, came from me, you were given everything, yet gave everything away; I hated you for bringing my head into this unacceptable way that you chose and will forever live with, but am done after this night.

The damp cool basement during the humid summers was the perfect place for you. I remember helping you get your things down into the new room for the first time. You smiled, you laughed, you came close to sharing yourself with me, but there was something that kept you from it. The way you changed after the move, convinced me that there are demons in the world. They are just waiting to take people over, to eat their souls, to devour the energy dwelling inside. And after you joined the confines of our cellar, you fully became one; I've come to terms with it, even if most are struggling in the belief.

Tim Eagle

I thought you had stopped because I quit finding things. I thought it was a phase and that you'd grown out of. I was so naïve. Having children brings a certain blinder to the eyes, it takes away any doubt in life, and coming to terms with how parenthood makes it more complicated when there is a struggle of this proportion to deal with. I tried taking advice from my church friends, even though I had stopped going to church at that point, it didn't help.

I tried to meditate, pray, tried other religions, but there was nothing to shake me awake!

Then, like everyone does in their life at some point, I found a book. It wasn't the Bible, like my friends suggested. It was a weirdly bound book that appeared next to me when I woke from a nap.

I was so frustrated with you that I began taking naps, long drawn out naps that helped my stress. It was a relief because I'd never been a daytime sleeper. My days became shorter because sleep would help me cope, help me dream, clear the conscious effort of you that was always in the forefront. I read the book, in all of its weird text, and didn't understand the large words, the weird things it spoke, but it was all the stuff that fills the mind. The things written in this book helped bring clarity, a lot like the naps did. It woke a part of my mind, which had slept for so long. It was that primitive part of my brain, the part that all of religion, all my beliefs, both traditionally and from the Christian faith, faded, and were replaced with something else entirely.

The book, in so many words helped guide me to that deep recess that we all should take a break from, and it brought clarity to the muddied truth I was facing. In my head, you were a killer, and I needed to stop you, everything I read in the book, convinced me further. Murder, incest, rape, cannibalism, the book was filled with it all, masked behind fiction, masked behind those sins that most blind themselves from. It absorbed me so much that I escaped into it, re-read it, memorized parts of it, lapped it up like the hungry savant of books that had left me when I got married. It was the first book that had ever come into my life that made sense, though the words were sinful, lustful, and filled with such a breed of nihilism, it took hold of me, made me whole again. My once guilt over hating you vanished with the nourishment those words offered me.

I was awake for the first time in many years!

Naps were replaced by reading and the desire to dig into you. More than anything, to understand the reasons, the rationale, and to understand where your desires came from, whether they were choices you opted for, or was it a genetic disposition from your father or me? I didn't know, and the clarity I had, was getting dim, the further time unfolded fate.

Spoken words were never right with me. I was never social enough to quite understand the plight that other women faced during parenthood, so I had only to rely on my best judgement, your father, and loose dialogue spoken in social circles. None of it helped. But the book soothed my worries, and it fed me knowledge that I never had before.

I woke from a nap, those little cat naps that had gone to the wayside when I started reading, and I heard the ringing from downstairs. It wasn't a bell; I didn't recognize it. It was echoing from the cistern in our cellar. The cistern was away from your room, at first I thought it was coming from your room, but it wasn't, the closer to the cistern I moved, the ringing stopped. There was a faded green light that eddied downward and into the depths of the endless pit, and then I heard a splashing that rang echoed off the sides.

Before I stood back to listen again, something growled, and the ringing started back up, then a growl, and the ringing stopped. I almost lost my bowel; I stood back, frozen in fear, because I heard of the myths and the legends of the old basements in Stevats. Those cisterns could give truth; they could conjure energy from within. There was something in the salt of the ground that mixed with the rain water, and created an abundance of energy, and once wished upon, the truth would be revealed.

I wished hard, through clenched teeth and eyes shut. Through the fear that had coursed through me to the moment I heard something wet smack the concrete. I opened slowly to the truth in front of me. As I slowly peeled my eyes open there was nothing, so much for the fanatics of the world, and all the lies feeding them.

While I was down in the damp moldy cellar and you weren't home, I went to your room.

The door squeaked behind me, my eyes fluttered at the light coming in through the windows and I reached under your bed. It was bizarre. I grabbed something from underneath. It was a hand. I pulled it out and attached to the hand was an arm. Both made of clay. I was elated, but didn't believe these weren't real human limbs. I fished for more, and there was a leg. It was fleshier than most, but still made of undried clay.

The wet sloshing smack of something outside the bedroom wall began slowly toward the open door. Dark began creeping in from outside. I froze again, this time bowel releasing and running down my leg. It was there, standing before me, a horror with no arms, just a scaly green slimy head with two piercing red eyes. Its feet two stumpy clumps at the end of appendages that was wet and beaded with water. There was not a mouth, just two holes under the eyes, one directly beneath each red eye that the thing took raspy inhalations with. I stood, again unable to move and the creature turned its back to me. Your face was embedded on its back, your eyes closed, your mouth in the shape of an "O" and a scream, as high pitch as it could be escaped. Your lips began to move.

"Mom, you did this to me, you did this to me, I was an artist, you were the killer, don't you remember! You taught me to be me, you taught me to stay away don't you remember?"

You quieted and became still, unlike my racing heart.

My head spun, memories fluttered through like a flash of fragments. I still couldn't recollect, but as I looked down at my hands, which I hadn't looked down to in quite some time, I saw my flesh stained with blood. My fingernails were caked beneath with dirt and excrement. I screamed, and the creature turned from me, sloshing back along the same path that it came. I heard it take the plunge into the dark waters of the cistern.

I changed, for the worse.

I lost faith, and you lost life, by my hands. The truth was revealed, now it's my time to reveal it to the world.

Tim Eagle

My mind is whole again, I AM AWAKE!

*

The audience was still, on my final words. I left the podium, the mask still irritating my skin, and walked away, down the other end of the stage. The fire crackled in hunger as I fed my mask to the flames. It was time to leave, to get out of this place where I found death, and a way to conceal it. My head had been playing games with me my whole life, hiding the real me through sleep. I was an addict, an addict to life, and to ending each and every ounce of energy it possessed. I will hide, and never be caught, I will live, but never truly live, I will hate, and hate with all my soul. Why? Because that's just what my life has always been, has always slept through, and will always be!

Flock

A large flock of hawks flew over Stevats before the storm. Avis Lark looked upward as the birds flew with stealth, hell bent in a southwesterly destination. He'd never known hawks to fly in a flock. They were hunters, birds of prey. He hoped there would be an article in the Stevats' Chronicle to explain it but wouldn't hold his breath. The Chronicle lacked Avis' standards of intellectual reading, and usually covered small-issues for small minds.

A dark growth of clouds was quickly moving in from the southwest, consuming the blue sky and sun overhead. There was a spit of moisture in the air. Avis debated on whether to go in to escape the coming storm. He stood by the shed which was home to a craftsman lawnmower and a weed trimmer; tools he intended to use but would not get around to because thunder spoke, encouraging him to leave.

The house was silent and held something ethereal,

something that didn't settle right. It pulled Avis into a desperate vortex and groped him as he tried hard to shove it all away. The living room was empty. Just one chair remained in the corner, a worn red plaid pattern settled into its fabric, its core, and the ass dent in the center called out to Avis, *"sit here, relax."* After his rounds through the house, shutting windows and pulling mini blinds, he took the chair's advice and sat down.

It was funny that in the genesis of relaxation, events and rifts of another time visited like whispering ghosts. The spirits chilled and an obscured atmospheric aura painted a bold picture. Ancient things—ideas, memories—chanted in melancholic waves and requiem, Avis sat up quickly, his equilibrium, like a teeter totter dominated by someone heavier, wobbled, and he fell to the floor. A stench of rotting compost, and earth, something unreal—*dead*—gripped him. He pushed up from the hard oak floor and wiped drool off the corner of his mouth.

Avis…

It was spoken in a distant, whispering melody that was close to being recognizable. It sounded like his wife Vanessa, but it had been so long ago that the familiarity of it was blurred. Avis' heart raced. He couldn't breathe.

Tears slipped out of an eye, falling like a river down Avis' cheek and a flash flood of hot memories ran laps like a rare film through an even more obsolete movie projector how it seemed so long ago. He took a deep breath and remembered someone. Her name was Tamara, Tamara Schlep.

*

Visceral, a gut wrenching conscious-ness Tamara was to

any man she crossed. She had been a long legged beauty, high cheek bones, a shape like the hourglass Avis' wife had lost after childbirth, and an ass that burned itself into every man's masturbatory recollection. Avis had been sucked into her web. He'd often played the fool, the village idiot at work because he hated his job, and Tamara had lured him in.

Tamara flirted, and he had flirted back. They met after work, sometimes spending nights together. He had known Tamara's womanly pink peach, shaven, and her long slender legs as smooth as polished chrome, like a road map. He was into a routine of pleasure when she left him. Tamara was using him and had milked him senseless.

After Tamara's departure Avis came back to life with the dullards, the grunts, and the worker bees of life. She had left a note that deflated his ego. He joined his family again and passed his wife often like a forlorn ship in the night. Life turned around when Vanessa, his wife of many forgotten years, rejuvenated with a burst of freak passion that Avis had given up on after kid number three.

Avis had not understood where the invigoration came from, just before the affair, Vanessa wouldn't give him the time or day and he'd be lucky to have sex once a month. It had been good to be back to the old days. Their marriage bloomed like it had been in the beginning, before the years of contempt and complacency.

*

Avis was sucked back into the lonely confines of the living room. The flash flood of memories cut him deep in his sullen demure. The recliner and the empty room greeted him shaking his hand and welcoming him back to the solitude of home. He took it in good measure and gimped to the recliner.

Avis had always been the despondent father and husband, extroverted dummy at work, introvert at home like so many other men in the world's fading work force. He was going through the motions, he had followed suite to everybody else but there were still monsters hiding in the nooks of his brain, secrets of dark matter, and the monsters waited patiently, obscured by the secret's confinement. Their breath was warm and the whispers were far from soothing. Little shitty droppings were left there to ferment like cough drops waiting to sooth a scratchy throat. The empty living room reflected what he deserved but to remember how it had become so barren, boggled him. He tried to remember the last time he saw Vanessa and the children, when had they left?

*

The affair, the renewal of sex and the small paychecks that had barely paid the bills; the miniscule amount of savings was always transferred to cover overdraft fees, rather than saved. The tiny gray hairs in the black hair of his head had begun to glimmer in streaks of silver as the Gods of age poured salt down from the heavens. Crow's feet spread at the corners of his eyes. He remembered slowly trying to morph himself into something else by working out, to compensate for old age that crept up on him faster than what he expected.

While he was tangled in the crisis of the thorny path of midlife, the phone had rung off the hook with bill collectors. The school called regularly about how the kids had been acting out. Avis' blood pressure had gone through the roof, his mind spun and he woke one morning from a deep sleep, assuming he had been sleep walking, standing outside next to his lawn equipment. The house was empty, his wife and kids left him with it all. The air was stale, blatantly stale. It didn't take a blood hound to know something was wrong, something that Avis sadly overlooked.

The hawks, where'd they come from? Didn't all of that just happen, the wakening, the flock peppering the sky? Avis thought.

*

He sat up, not realizing he had nodded off in the chair, still confused about how things had changed in his life. His head spun and the darkness of a loud storm veiled outside blackening the living room. The pounding of thunder rattled the house, shook wall hangers, that once held family pictures, and Avis fell to the floor. He didn't have the strength to push up this time and was overwhelmed by the stench of compost, and earth, something unreal, *dead* made his legs freeze. He tried to reposition, but to no avail. As he twisted his upper body the floor board beneath the weight creaked in song, and chills blanketed him. A tingling sensation of cold air lifted the small hairs on the back of his neck. They were like spider legs coming to life wriggling like foreign appendages.

A second floor board creaked.

Enough feeling returned to Avis' legs to move from the singing oak floor boards and he lifted them. It looked like someone removed the boards and replaced the nails with something inferior than what originally held them down. With gritted teeth he slowly revealed cobwebs, the joist that supported the floor, and dank earth below. He squinted to see and could only make out dark anonymity of the house's crawlspace.

He stuck his head into the abyss, the stench stung his eyes, and bile rose into the back of his throat. Beneath the house the old wiring dangled large sixty watt light bulbs and the air flow of the living room jostled them, he heard one smash against a joist board that it was attached to and the other lights flickered. Squinting and trying to breathe through only his mouth, something creamy and fleshy caught his eye, the lights went out.

It was probably just a grub or something. Avis thought lifting his head from the darkened cave.

Yellow ambient light flickered on again and Avis took in a breath and stuck his head back down with his eyes closed. He feared the dark, feared the unknown species of creeping crawling spiders that lurked in the hidden crevices of an alien space. The lights didn't go out, but the breath from Avis Lark's lungs left quickly as he slowly opened his eyes. Staring with rotting gelatinous sockets was an almost cleaned skull. Long skeletal bones of a hand rested next to the skull and on the ring finger a sapphire glimmered faintly by the lights. Avis dry heaved.

The skull belonged to Tamara; the sapphire ring was hers.

Avis tried to remember. *Did he kill her?*

His mind was flustered and flitted like barren wings. As if he were bobbing for apples he took in a deep breath and stuck his head back into the hole. This time he wasn't greeted by the sapphire ring but another skull a foot from Tamara's.

Avis' muscles stopped moving, and his eyes froze on the skull, next to it a hand holding the Stevats' Chronicle. The headline: *A Large Flock of Hawks*...below the headline was a picture of hawks with the blue back drop of sky and a trace of dark storm clouds directly behind them. His eyes moved from the paper to the half fleshy skull staring at him. Maggots' bright white in the yellow glow crawled in and out of the skull, a putrid smell wafted...his wedding band was missing but glimmered on the corpses hand as the lights slowly faded into a flood of memory and an inundation of fear and understanding that he was dead...

*

Avis was hurled into the sight of a flock flying overhead. The weed trimmer spun from behind him. He was so enthralled by the flying flock of hawks that he mistook the noise as his neighbor's mowing. Avis' eyes were squinted into two slits trying to gather the marvel of floating hawks. A leader hawk screeched and several other noises followed alien noises humming, whizzing, foreign sound from the neighbor's house. The weed trimmer spun faster and closer but Avis' head was still titled like a sunflower's towards the sky, disregarding the buzz. His mouth hung open and he had every intention to call the kid's out to see the birds but couldn't because he didn't want to miss a second of it. The swirling hawks were like dozens of kites flying for the first time in the spring.

Avis' noticed the open shed door but didn't notice that his own weed trimmer wasn't in the shadows. It was not a big deal because the shed wasn't wired for lighting and he must have overlooked it. He cherished the tool so much but the intrigue of birds in the blue sky had taken it all away.

His weed trimmer was more of a twig chopper, it wasn't string fed. It was a hard bladed whipper that Avis modified. There were three metal blades attached to the spool at the end, each carved with grooves like the blade of a reciprocating saw. Avis customized it for the high growth of bushes that bordered his property and the farmland surrounding his yard. The weed whipper was equipped to handle any small saplings that stood in its way; it ate through wood like an overgrown termite in need of sustenance.

A faint familiar smell of the lilac perfume Vanessa liked to wear tinted the gasoline and oil mix. Avis turned around...

The sting felt like a bee, the slice unfelt because it was done with stealth and had cut through his jugular. Avis saw his blood paint a bizarre mural onto the cement which oddly looked like the spread of India ink he had done when he was a small boy. Falling to his knees, his head lolled and dangled on the axis, he saw the wide white grin of Vanessa and the customized tree chopper dripping with red. His vision spun as Vanessa grabbed the head and snapped it; he toppled with a thud.

Vanessa peered down at Avis, her sneer plastered to the face like a still photo shoot. She let a slow breath out beneath her teeth and hissed taking in another. Her lips quivered and she spoke, "You should've been better, Avis. I expected more from you. Why did you fuck around on me?"

Avis' eyes grew heavy and the lids darkened sight like a funeral pall, he took one last breath...

*

A large flock of hawks flew over Stevats before the storm. Avis stood by the shed which was home to the craftsman lawnmower and a weed trimmer, tools he intended to use but never got around to. Thunder spoke first, so Avis scurried inside, history and the memories all just lost snippets forgotten, but looping endlessly.

Poco

Do you think the end is near? Have you craved the zany theories of a solar planetary line up that's going to shift the earth's magnetic poles, screwing us all? Putting on Nike Air, drinking some water to digest the old seizure meds and hopping aboard a comet, just because some nut job tells you that Jesus is waiting for you on the comet? Then you know how my life is every day. My life is lonely, too much time to think. I want, therefore I am unwanted. Ever hear of that? Probably not, it's just something I like to say.

Poco is my name, Poco Galypto. Sometimes, if I let my mind get sucked into the vortex of the idea that all success and determination is in a name, I get a little funny, because it rings so close to home. My name is like my life, lame. I'm a Caucasian—Greek with a Spanish name, that's all I have to say about it.

Driving was always my saving grace. I drove to get away from it all. I drove to get away from my mom's home cooking, which contributed to my belt line protrusion and made me look nine months pregnant from the right visual angle. I drove to get away from my damp basement bedroom. But most of all, I drove just to listen to music and disappear into the melodious sound of eighties hits. I melted away in the car, wishing I were on stage playing the bass, playing lead, or jamming on the drums. All those things were just fantasy to me, but they helped kill time. I worked and that was another place I disappeared. It would allow me to escape the self-created confines of life that often suffocate.

I was a courier for Suncrest Memorial Lab. I picked up blood specimens, fecal specimens, urine, and pap smears. I collected them from physician's offices, other smaller hospitals, and clinics and brought them to the home lab for processing. My job was simple, boring, yet entertaining and paid all of my bills.

Being a courier had its perks; for one thing I could drive and better still, people left me alone. The only bother, and it was sporadic throughout my eight-hour day, were calls from the phone bank and lab's triage area. They'd call, tell me that there was a STAT specimen needing picked up forcing me to re-route. Most couriers took breaks in their cars. I preferred a change of scenery and visited the heated smoke shack behind the Billing department.

The smoke shack was the place to hear all the gossip. I heard who was sleeping with who, who everyone liked, who everyone would likely vote off the show of life, if life were just reality television and everyone was playing to win a million dollars. I listened to it all, absorbing it like a sponge. The faint whisper came from the corner of the hovel where secrets took place, the stuff no one wanted an outsider like me to know.

I was determined to hear it all so I bought one of those magic ears advertised on QVC, a show I always watched with my Mom. She pried and asked why I was ordering it and I lied telling her it was to hear conversations better over the Nextel phone that base called me on. She fell for it. It was that magic ear that let me in on the darker side of gossip.

I understood the reason why people gossiped, it was to make them feel better. I just didn't get why they always picked on the lonely people like me. Those who worked hard, but didn't like to fit in, those who liked to keep their personal lives personal. It was one of life's mysteries I didn't care to know, because the juice this time was not me, it was R.J Bigger.

What I gathered about R.J. is that he was despised by people and was most avoided in the office on a constant measure. It was the way he'd always beg for rides from people or mooch cigarettes or food for lunch. Hearing this, I was sad for the guy; I never met him before but knew who he was because he ambled into the smoke shack. Everyone smoking stopped talking put their cigarettes out and looked in the other direction or shuttled out the door.

The smell of R.J. was of sour buttermilk and cat shit and that didn't bother me. It was the way he limped into the smoke shack and the way everyone then ignored one of their own that did bother me. I needed to find out more about him. He seemed harmless enough, pleasant enough, smiling crookedly, with missing teeth, at everyone. The fluorescent lights glimmering off his bald head resembled a halo; Mom always told me that people needed to treat others like Jesus did. I couldn't figure out why the hatred and ignorance was going on toward R.J, there was something simple about him. That was the connection I had with him, I was simple, at least that was what my Mom always told me, "You're simple Poco, that's just what people will have to get used to," Mom had no reason to lie to me, so R.J was an interesting connection.

After working, I parked my courier's car, turned in my keys and Nextel phone. I proceeded to my car where I listened to The Conquering Worms, not too loud, because I didn't want attention. Billing personnel worked till five o'clock so I had about an hour and a half to kill. I enjoyed a small snack, a value sized bag of Frito Lay chips, and a two liter of grape Faygo. It was delicious. Mixed with some good music it was the closest thing to being home.

As I guzzled the rest of the two liter, R.J. ambled out into the parking lot. I almost didn't recognize him with his winter hat on; if it weren't for the limp he could have slipped right past, unnoticed. He was smiling and I knew right away why. Walking next to him was Kim one of the billing supervisors. She had long legs and wore tight fitting business attire. A long Virginia Slim hung from her middle and index finger. Her smile was filled with straight rows of pearly whites; two fine dimples dented the tips of her smile. R.J. was rambling on and on, I could see white plumes of cold air billow out of his mouth as his lips ranted what seemed a mile a minute. He had a certain glow, a gleam in his eyes.

Three cars down and across from my Focus was a black Taurus and the parking lights flashed when Kim unlocked it. The couple got in. I was ready to follow but I had to wait for Kim to start her car before I started mine so it would cover for me. I wasn't doing anything wrong, but I didn't want bad rumors about stalking, so I kept a low profile.

I saw the tail lights leave and followed at a safe distance. Stevats was dying down for the evening. Businesses usually shut down at four thirty, but the industrial park was letting the day shift go and I blended into the cars of the factory rats. Not enough traffic to cause a backup, but just enough for me to stay behind Kim and R.J. at a distance. My stomach rumbled from nerves, from excitement, from doubt, maybe from the Faygo and Fritos. Something told me that I had to reach out to R.J. I couldn't take everyone else's judgment and think so little of a man that everyone hated. I brushed the negative thoughts away.

City limits ended and the houses were scattered fragments of civilization. Kim turned down Stevats' County Road. Maybe he and Kim were having a fling. I knew that R.J. was a single man, but Kim, she flaunted her large diamond wedding ring in the tarnished yellow light of the smoke shack. She always talked about how happy she was with her husband. The whole R.J./Kim thing cast a web of enigmatic proportion and drew me deeper into the intrigue.

The Taurus swerved across the left lane and back into the right. The brake lights' crimson glow shone when the car pulled over to the shoulder. The brake lights dimmed and the car began to rock. I continued to drive passed them. I glanced fast to not draw attention and Kim was nowhere to be seen. R.J. was in the passenger seat as the dome light faded off. The car began rocking from side to side, up and down. Slightly aroused I pulled to the side of the road. I was sweating, had to piss, and had a mad urge to bust a U'ie and drive away. I had to pull it together, get my head straight. Were they just bumping uglies?

I eased into the thought of my Mom's Friday meatloaf dinner, and gathered my senses. Chances of them recognizing me were slim so I turned the car around. If I caught something that I wasn't supposed to catch, say, maybe Kim's head bobbing up and down on R.J. or getting undressed in the back seat it wasn't obvious by the couple in their confines. I needed to go home, I'd seen enough. My pity for R.J. disappeared.

Pulling out and driving back by was a bad idea. R.J. had got out of the car. There was enough daylight left to emphasize a clown red smile painted around his lips. He waved slowly; his hands were stained with red, too thick to be paint. The Frito's and Grape Faygo almost tumbled from my stomach and in thick vomit out onto the steering wheel. I swear there were strings of skin caught in the gap between his large two front teeth. I sped by and raced home. Terror had settled in and the deep sense that I may have been witness to something gruesome was a difficult truth to swallow.

I couldn't go to the cops, what if R.J. and Kim were just kinky and got dressed up? Maybe my overactive, un-stimulated imagination conjured it all? I had the weekend to think it over. I wasn't in the right frame of mind to visit the cops, they were busy enough handling vandalism at the cemetery, dead people, missing people, molested children, how could I bother them with my paranoia?

There was a note left for me when I got home, my parents and brother had gone shopping, meatloaf was in the oven, I ate my fill with a pile of mashed potatoes. After dinner, I nestle into my bedroom with my laptop and began recounting the scenes. There was nothing in Stevats that would excite me this much and I wished hard to forget it all.

I'm alone, trying to cross all my "t's" and dot all my "i's". I could just delete this file and be done with it, wipe it away permanently, but something's telling me that one day it just may be important.

One thump comes from upstairs. Two thumps, a pause, and then the same pattern. There's breath outside the thin hollow door blocking my room from the stairs.

I hear the old rusty hinges groan from behind me. Fear revisits me and my heart races, and as I'm typing this into my laptop, I don't know if I should turn around to see who it is. The breathing is heavy, thick and wet. It's probably just my brother, wait a minute, my laptop is one of those old ones that don't block the glare of lights, and it doesn't dim the screen for privacy. I see the glimmer of something steel, I see a reflection of someone with red painted lips standing behind me, shit I think its R.J. I should have gone to the...

There will be Tears

There was love, but with it came terror running toward me from the woods. I leapt away from the bleeding creature. Blood, thick large streams, dribbled down the deranged, what appeared to be, woman's chin. She sneered; her teeth biting down on her lower lip, her eyes were two slits of anger, and her pupil's red bulbs popping out of her head. I almost shit my pants. She looked away briefly so I pumped my legs and ran as fast as I could.

Her name was Tearelle. I needed to get away from her, because it looked like she had been on a killing spree. There was something about the furl of red painted around her lips that terrified me. I came upon an abandoned house. Peeling paint and missing gingerbread whispering the fading hymn of glories past. The decaying porch was the nearest shelter I could see so I dove through the fence of towering weeds into the cool musty shade. It smelled of cat piss and rotting wood it was so much better than facing the mad woman. She moved slowly down the street toward the Victorian, searching.

*

Tearelle used to be an aide at Stevats Memorial in the Central Processing Center of the lab. She was terminated for calling in sick too often. She had hated me from the moment she started working there. I overheard enough of other's conversations in the smoke shack to know she hated me, for reasons I never knew, some souls were never meant to be in this life.

I was part of a small group at work. There weren't many of us, just the few who enjoyed words and repeated them until the word burned itself into our co-worker's brains. We drank together; often playing word games, usually creating synonyms for work related terms or functions. Our party nights were few and far between because the guys and I were family men. We'd hang at the Softtail Saloon once a month and were limited to that.

Some time ago, before Tearelle was around, I don't remember exactly when, Jim Grogan, Chuck Krutz and me were processing, a tube of synovial fluid, joint fluid. It fell down the pneumatic tube structure with a hiss and landed with a thump. The fluid looked like a runny pink yogurt in a pointed tube, sort of like peaches and cream baby food. The sight of it actually turned my stomach but the word I used bubbled deep within and sounded so alien coming out that Chuck laughed and Jim followed suite. It became a routine; whenever synovial fluid would come into the lab, we would all say, "Nom-Nom-Nom." We sounded like a barber shop quartet feeding a baby in a high chair.

One day, the repetitious "nom-nom-nom," erupted and Tearelle snapped. She stomped out of the basement and through the hospital mumbling angrily. The guys and I had a good chuckle over it and that was that. We didn't hear anything from her, or see her again—at work anyway.

I had already forgotten about the odd, humorless woman until I saw her next. My youngest, Jimmy, and I were walking down Main Street.

She was driving a white Geo Tracker down the deserted street and stopped in the middle of the road, brakes hollering and squealing. Tearelle rolled down the driver's side window, and stared at me through a set of cheap sunglasses. Her face was as red as her large bulbous nose, as if she had been drinking. A wide grin exposed a large set of teeth and she screeched, "Nom-nom-nom!" It was high pitched, chilling almost.

I expected a punch line, something, anything. She stared empty through those dark shades and sped off. I could hear the gears shift frantically. My youngest looked up to me, rolled his eyes and shrugged his shoulders. It was obvious she had a bad case of job envy.

*

Time seemed to have paused beneath the porch. Tearelle walked slowly, awkwardly up the front steps and plopped onto an old swing. Did she know I was hiding? Was she going to play cat and mouse with me until I came out from underneath the porch? I knew better than to fall for it. My bladder began to scream because I took a three p.m. coffee break at work, just an hour and a half before quitting time. The coffee had run its course. It was either piss myself or risk being caught. Tearelle stopped swinging as the warm liquid seeped out and soaked into my Khakis, it was as if she could hear the dribble from where she sat. Relieved but ashamed, I cringed as the warm-piss turned cold and began working on chaffing my legs.

A hearty chuckle left the crazy lady's throat and for the first time since the chase began, she spoke, "Nom-nom-nom. My work is done. Nom-nom-nom" I could hear her dry hands rubbing together and the porch singing under her weight as she left.

She walked east in the direction of Maple Street heading toward my house. My stomach fluttered, adrenaline pumped, I scattered out from my dirty hiding space at a sprint, but her madness made her faster.

*

Since Tearelle got fired, things at work were strange and hazy. The group I had formed dissolved. I still kept the momentum. It was the way things in my life were, go to bed, get up, go to work, come home and repeat, what was in a word? When life got dull, I spruced it up with vigor. I began getting mean looks from people, they snarled at me instead of greeting me in the morning and the mental beating became too much.

I surrendered, submitted, something I rarely did in life and shut up. If people hated me for being a parrot, they hated me, but the oddest was the fact that my buddies from the group had been like me. They were non-quitters of our created annoyances. Before I would completely crawl into an introverted role, I confronted Chuck. He would come clean and tell me what was going on.

I walked to the specimen triage area, the place where the pneumatic tubes would deliver, where Chuck worked, "Can you talk?"

"Sure, the in-patient stuff is slow right now, must be lunch time on the floors."

"Let's step over here." I walked; he followed me to an area off stage.

"What's up?" Chuck asked. He had a puzzled almost panicked look on his face.

"The whole, nom-nom-nom, thing, you guys haven't said it in a while. You're all acting a little funny. All the years we've done the word thing, I've never known one of you to back off from it the way you have," I explained.

"It's a long story, Jim," he said. His eyes kept looking down at his crotch. I didn't want to follow because I thought he was just screwing around and trying to get me to take a glance, I refused.

He was not bluffing, and not a smirk touched his lips. His gaze was cold, stone. "Just a hint," I asked.

Chuck's eyes darted back down to his crotch and I wouldn't follow.

"Meet me in the bathroom as soon as Kim covers my lunch."

"Sure, but why the bathroom, are you too good for the cafeteria?" I asked reluctantly agreeing, even though the crotch reference followed by an invitation to the bathroom was a little disturbing.

"It's there or nothing," Chuck's voice was flat.

The tubes began dropping, I left the triage area and back into the processing cubicle to type more registrations. Half an hour later Chuck walked by and I followed with that same disinclination.

He stood in the bathroom. His eyes were large and his mouth moved a mile a minute, "She's fucked us all, Jim, take a look. I can't be long, she'll know, she's got spies everywhere. If she finds out, my wife is going to kill me."

"Slow down, Chuck. Tell me what the fuck's going on."

Chuck rolled up his sleeve and exposed his hairy arm. Two bloody "S's" were carved into it. And he winced when his long sleeve rubbed against the raw letters.

"What the hell, where the hell, what does it mean, who did it?"

"It was Tear…" the bathroom door swung open and Chuck spun to the sink pretending to wash his hands rolling his sleeve back down. He didn't have to finish explaining, I had put the pieces together, the mystery wasn't completely solved, but where it was going drove me nuts. It was Tearelle, the same shit she did to Jimmy and me when we were walking to the hardware store, only it had played out on the physical level with Chuck.

I got the chills walking out of the bathroom and couldn't look at anyone after I saw the raw red flesh on Chuck's arm. I didn't think Tearelle was finished.

*

My house was dark as I approached. There were no lights on except for the foyer in the back. I was sweating and my heart thumped so hard that I thought I was going to puke. I hoped Tearelle didn't beat me home. All was silent behind me and the neighborhood kids were all heading home.

I couldn't muster the strength to run. If there was a weapon of any kind in Tearelle's hands I could be mutilated. I took cautious baby steps and saw a large dark shadow move in the foyer's light and cascade over the lawn outside, Tearelle was in the house. I hunkered beneath a bush; erratic movements of the behemoth that infiltrated the house flitted around on the patch of yellow light like an array of dark puzzle pieces.

She exited the foyer and I quietly bounced up the back porch, cautiously opened the door and was shocked at all the blood. Shaky words were scrawled like alien hieroglyphs on the bright yellow paint. I almost puked.

The words were fleshy little clumps clinging in sections that rolled to the floor in a slow snowball tumble. The blood was hot, wet and fresh on the paint. The words like searing, mocking revenge: *NOM-NOM-NOM!*

A large clump of vomit burned the back of my throat. I heard the television on upstairs and the kids were laughing and the wife was talking, not one of them knew Tearelle had been in the house. From out of nowhere Tearelle stood in front of me. Her meaty arms down to her sides and dangling from her large left hand was a serrated knife and in the right a branding iron.

"Well, well, well," She said. Her smile was zany, insane. The look in her eyes wild, her pupils dilated.

"Tearelle," I said.

She clicked her tongue at me and freeing an index finger from the knife told me to silence. "It's my turn now, Jim; the balls are in my court, quite literally," her eyes gazed down at my crotch. "If you're quiet, very quiet, you can hear why you should mind your p's and q's."

Fear and anger stirred and the maddening pressure to bolt at this deranged creature surged. Her smile was crooked; she had filed her teeth into sharp incisors.

"No funny business, Jim." She pocketed the knife and touched the branding iron to the carpet. It sizzled and black smoke emitted a putrid stench. "I can give you this on the arm, like your good friends and you can abide by my rules to end it all."

She stood in front of me. Her teeth glimmered in the ambient light. I quivered, she was winning. I surrendered. "What, what is it you're going to do to my family if I don't abide by your rules?"

"I kill them all." She was like a magician and instead of pulling a rabbit out of her hat she pulled a small blinking remote control from another pocket. The red light flashed steadily, "I press this button and blow them into pieces."

"You'll kill all of us."

"Jim, Jim, Jim, it's just a small blast, one that would level the upper floor, splatter the flesh of your wife and kids over the charred boards. The only thing that will bother us...well, you, would be the smell of a human roast."

Vomit rose in my throat, I was strapped for words, strapped for any other solution other than endure the hot branding iron on my arm like Chuck had to.

"You're giving me a choice, right?" I asked.

"Do you want the tattoo and to save your family?" She sneered. "I'm losing my patience here."

"Save them." I closed my eyes and held out my arm. The smell of carpet had been nothing compared to the burning melting smell of my skin as Tearelle branded me. Two bloody "S's" were swelling on my arm like a child's scribble and tears ran down my face.

"You now belong to me," Tearelle said. I opened my eyes and she was naked. Two lumpy fat breasts and stomach greeted me like an albino whale had beached itself in my house.

"What the fuck are you doing now? I did what you asked."

"Everything but," Tearelle pointed down to her hairy bush half covered by her stomach, "You belong to me, you're my *Sex Slave*."

*

I passed out, faded to black, and remembered waking to my family around a hospital bed at Stevats' Memorial. My wife and kids stood with smiles and tears as they showered me with balloons, flowers and hospital gifts. They explained to me that I'd be in the hospital for a while and left me to get rest and get better. As the television news droned and my eyelids grew heavy I began to pass out and the door opened.

There was a rush of air as my blanket was taken off. I thought it had been the wife paying me a nightly rendezvous and was surprised by a fat woman sitting on top of me and humping. I felt her rough calloused fingers smoothly run over the branding on my forearm. I wanted to scream but through my squinting eyes could see a bright red light rapidly blinking on a remote.

"Oh," she moaned, "You've turned into quite the naughty slave—NOM-NOM-NOM." The words were the whispered incantation of a mad woman.

The pain in my groin and the newly introduced

agony had haunted me with repetition. With love there was terror and it would fill every second of life to come.

Tea for Two

Life is but a box. The lid opens and allows one to see the light, like that of heaven or that which a newborn sees leaving the womb and entering the world. The lid closes and darkness resides deep within, hiding in the corners like ghosts are memories, cowering in the crushed velvet lining something real. The box is light weight but carries the burden of an undisclosed past. Vivian Hendrix stared at her box, relished in her celebration to come, but had purged the historical secret within. Her mind and life are one in the same, a golden trinket, a velvet lined box, macabre memories that echo unheard, pushed away, and feared.

The box held intrigue; it held mystique and Vivian couldn't stop looking at it. Embedded in the gold exterior were lines scrolled delicately like road maps to another world, a world that Vivian often wished she were a part of. She contemplated what was inside, *knew* what *it* was inside of the box, but with all her will power would wait for the right moment to open it.

She stared at her computer. The tiny confines of a cubicle created a soft comfortable feel because of the intricately detailed box gazing at her. It taunted every eye movement, tantalized the working world where she was trying to create a memo for Mr. Dryer. She took in a deep breath, grabbed the box and ran her finger over the three dimensional roadmaps and the sunken valleys grooved in the metal. The cold metal of the container sent shivers up and down her back and she squirmed at *something* ethereally touching her.

"Vivian?" The voice came from behind her.

Vivian jumped and set the box down. She saw that it was Mr. Dryer. "I'm sorry, sir, just finished typing that memo for you. Is there anything else you had for me today?" Vivian gained composure quickly, she hoped that Mr. Dryer didn't think she was weird or even caught on to the moment she was having.

"No. I just wanted to wish you a happy birthday, that's all." Mr. Dryer smiled. He handed her an envelope. "Here's a little something for your longevity with us. It's not much."

"You didn't have to," Vivian started.

"No, don't say it. You, as well as everyone else here at Suncrest, make us who we are. We couldn't do it without you." Mr. Dryer said. His eyes were sincere, his actions genuine.

"Thanks, Mr. Dryer." Vivian said.

"You're welcome. If you're finished and want to head home for the day, that'd be fine by me, Vivian. Why don't you go celebrate your birthday?"

Butterflies churned in Vivian's stomach, she was

looking for an excuse to leave and Mr. Dryer gave her one, "That sounds good; I'll take you up on it." Vivian smiled. It was a fake smile, but a smile just the same.

"See you tomorrow," Mr. Dryer said on his way out of her cubicle. She could make out his balding head and few sparse hairs on the top over the cubicles as he walked away.

"Yep, see you tomorrow." Vivian said. She shoved the box in her pocket. A sense of warmth on her flesh enticed her further; she couldn't wait to get home. She closed out the files she had been working on, shut down her laptop and grabbed her coat. She put her gloves, hat and boats on to leave and double checked her cubicle. All was well.

Being lonely bothered Vivian. Her parent's death had left her with the gift of solitude, and it filled her with emptiness. Vivian walked out of the office. Computer screens lit everyone's faces and not one person turned to wish her a happy birthday or say good bye. That was fine by Vivian. She knew everything about all of them them, yet they knew nothing but superficial rumors of her. She wrapped her long fingers around the box in her pocket, took a deep breath and finished her walk.

Once she was outside the angst that had surfaced, subsided. Suncrest Nursing Home was at the top of Audubon Hill and Vivian had a few miles to make it to town. She zipped her coat up to the bottom of her chin and started home. She didn't drive, had never learned to drive. Her mom and dad always intended on teaching her, but never got around to it. Her parents were very busy people. They used to run a retail shop downtown Stevats and Vivian seldom saw them at home. When she did talk with them it was usually while she stocked shelves at the store.

The winding roads soothed Vivian. The ground was barren of snow; the last snow storm had all melted with a quick one day winter warm up, and the temperature was mild. Gray storm clouds filled the sky and the sun was a dim yellow spec behind the canvas. Dark gray woods emphasized the overcast in a lackluster demure. She ambled down the side of the road on a bike trail, safe from traffic. Vivian was soothed by the solitude of noiseless atmosphere. She relished in it.

Vivian didn't feel older, just a little wiser, and the self fulfilling promise she made to herself for her twenty-first birthday was to take a warm bath, open up a jug of sweet tea, and then open the gold box. Chills tingled up her back and raised the tiny hairs on her neck at the thought of the trinket box.

Down the winding bike path and curving through the shadows of large oak Vivian arrived at the bottom of Audubon Hill. She was greeted by several factories in an industrial park. Exhaust stacks emitted plumes of smoke that rose in the air and the smell was that of sugar beets being processed by a local sugar company. The scent was a fecal rotting smell. Vivian didn't mind it; she had grown accustom to it. She was born and raised in Stevats. It was second nature to experience the abhorrent stench.

Vivian passed the monolithic structure with the beacon of an American flag waving on top of one of the storage towers and a surge of anxiety riddled her. Her brother worked in one of those buildings and she hoped that he wasn't outside to spot her. Since her parent's deaths Vivian hadn't spoken to Sam. He lived his life and she hers. That's the way Vivian liked it. Her eyes darted in and out of the large piles of sugar beets. There was no one there, so she scurried like a rat past the factory and down to Main Street.

When you're twenty-one... A haunting voice of her past whispered.

Vivian shut it out because it wasn't a healthy voice and whispers frightened her. The busy downtown distracted her from the chilling whisper. People were shopping for Christmas, scurrying to their cars with groceries and getting last minute items before heading home from work. Vivian was jealous of the activity, but would not succumb to the foolishness. She was a black and white thinker, structure, routine and nothing beyond that spectrum ruled her life. She understood that life had only one line and that was a straight line, there were no alternative routes to follow, and there were no forks in the road, just a boring black line drawn down the center.

You took the fork in the road with me. The whisper chanted.

"Go away, I'm forgetting you," Vivian said. She hadn't realized she was speaking out loud until a passing shopper gave her a funny look.

The store fronts of downtown Stevats eventually faded and large two and three story Victorian homes lined the street. Most of these homes were made into apartments. Vivian was lucky to have an apartment downtown in one of the old Victorians. It was her first independent act of liberating from the confines of her childhood home.

Your move was a relief for you, but a pain for me,

sis. The voice returned.

Vivian wanted to scream. It was her brother's voice. She turned around to make sure he wasn't following her and bolted the rest of the way home. The thought of Sam scared her, someone who she avoided at all costs. Daddy wasn't around to save her from him.

In her apartment, Vivian's heart raced, her mind panicked, and muddied daylight seeped through the closed shades. She thought she saw something dash through the gray light. It was her shadow being cast over the couch. Relieved by her own paranoia she laughed and remembered the gold box in her pocket—exhilaration and joy!

"Almost time, sweets," She said. Vivian tapped the box in her pocket and put it on top of the television. Talking to the box put some life into her step, gave her some enthusiasm.

The box was an antique given by Vivian's mother when Vivian turned thirteen. It was a present to represent Vivian coming of age, the womanly age when a young girl begins her period. The inside was lined with soft, smooth red velvet. Vivian remembered caressing the lining when she opened it and relished how it felt on her fingertips. She sat down on the couch with a bottle of water.

Vivian's mother told her the symbolism of the box. The curvatures and roadmap was that of a young girl's life when she comes of age. The scrolls are the young girl's adventures, her goals, and her life line. The red lining inside represents life, which has been given and in return will be given back when the time is right. The box was sacred. Vivian nurtured the thoughts, the symbolism, and the poetry of the golden trinket box. Most of all the past voice of her mother, who wasn't arguing with Vivian's dad but showing Vivian that she loved her. It was that one on one time that Vivian liked to think about. She didn't like to think of mother as cold and distant, but held a normal relationship with Vivian and the memory allowed that illusion. Vivian had dosed off and woke abruptly startled that maybe she had lost the trinket.

The box was nested between her legs, she could feel its warmth, it was alive and it was almost time for her celebration. The wind outside her apartment howled. Through the shade Vivian could see snow falling. The snow had accumulated fast and a drab gray blanket swarmed over the sky and diminished any sign of sunlight.

The cool tile floor of the bathroom greeted her bare feet and sent chills up Vivian's legs. The side of the claw tub like ice as she knelt over it to start a warm bath. Steam condensed everything with fingers as the tub filled. She took her clothes off and held the box next to her face in the mirror. She smiled for the picture perfect moment. She slipped into the comforts of her warm bath and made sure not to get the box wet.

Vivian held the box in her left hand, which dangled over the side of the bathtub and her right hand rested on her leg. She thought back to how hard she worked through her primary school years and how the hard work paid off. Those memories were positive for her, she had dived into her school work, ran with her life, but there were always secrets buried. It was the secrets alone that terrified her because they were surreal moments in her history, blurred and blocked out, but at the moment sucked her into the macabre vortex. It was the gift she held, that sacred box that brought the memories back, and gave her confidence to endure them.

Vivian's mother and father worked hard in their store. It was always the same routine. Vivian would wake, shower and go to school. Her mom and dad would be gone. Two days after receiving the box, the routine changed. Vivian woke to her brother Sam next to her on the bed. She sat up quickly; between her legs something sticky. Sam smiled, his cheeks were bunched up, the freckles smashed together under his eyes, and he didn't say anything.

"Sam, what did you do?"

"I'm sorry, Vivian, I couldn't wait for you anymore." Sam pleaded. He was three years older than Vivian. Vivian was disgusted at what she felt on her inner thighs.

"What is this stuff," Vivian asked.

"I came. I'm sorry; tomorrow I'll be more careful. This is our secret." Sam whispered.

Vivian was infuriated, intimidated, and didn't know what to do. She had heard other girls talk about sex at school had even heard rumors that boys stick their thing inside of a girl's belly button to make babies. Vivian ran to the bathroom looked down at her belly button and saw clear viscous liquid dripping from it.

The act proceeded every night until eventually Sam got it right. Vivian wouldn't wake up with warm sticky fluid on her legs or belly button but felt it inside her and the raw itch of her private areas pained. Confused and with no one to turn to she dove deeper into her books and thought of the gold box that her mother gave her. She wished hard into the gold box, wished for a cure, wished for Sam to stop. After her homework and before settling into a good book she took the box out from underneath her pillow and opened it.

Vivian knew that her mother said the box had special powers. The box contained warmth of something else, the weight had changed. A wish, an answer to her thoughts, and an answer to her problem basked in the dim overhead light.

Vivian let the sexual abuse go on, not by choice but because she knew that Sam overpowered her. She slept through most of it because it was her only defense. She cringed when waking every morning at the smell of Sam inside of her and scrubbed trying to rid herself of him. She thought of the box more and more until it took away the pain of Sam molesting her. Thoughts took away the risks, the isolation and the lonliness that owned her.

On the night it all stopped Vivian was nervous, scared, every emotion that coursed through her ate her nerves. Vivian waited and then saw Sam's shadow pace outside the door like a hungry predator. The television in Vivian's mom and dad's room shut off and she heard her door open. She closed her eyes and held the box tightly out of sight.

Sam was fevered with heat as he climbed on top of Vivian, his weight heavy and overbearing. Vivian cringed as he slid his hand down her thighs and then himself into her. Puke rose in the back of her throat. He worked hard and fast, in and out until he finished. She slowly opened the box when Sam lifted himself off.

He stood at the end of her bed and his shadow like a

monster's cascaded over Vivian's timid eyes. A grin filled his face. Terrified Vivian pulled out a knife, the wish of Vivian's primal thoughts and survival, from the box. She could hear the silent giggle as Sam bounced up and down on the bed, could hear him whisper to her thinking she was asleep, his voice haunting and surreal. She stabbed blindly in the dark and heard his scream. The blade hit something hard as it sliced through his flesh. Like magic the knife crunched through a bone. The last she remembered as she threw herself from the bed to get away was commotion in the hall. It was Vivian's father screaming.

Vivian cleaned up a bloody mess and slept the rest of the night. She heard the news of Sam the next morning. He was in the hospital and had lost his large toe on his right foot. Vivian's mother explained to Vivian that Sam had an accident with some buddies and that her dad would be home after the surgery. It was the one and only time that Vivian remembered the shop closing.

The abuse had stopped, but there were plenty of verbal threats from Sam. Eventually everything worked out for the better as Sam moved on with his life. Vivian distanced herself from him as he did with the entire family. The words that Sam whispered in pain the night Vivian lobbed off his toe were, *"When you're twenty-one, you better celebrate, because I'll see you to your grave."*

Vivian's bath water turned cold, gooseflesh crawled on her skin as Sam's voice haunted her. Outside the wind sang with the snow and a *thud* came from the stairs. She dressed in her red silk pajamas, set out two tea cups and the jug of sweet tea reserved for the occasion. She grabbed two cupcakes from the refrigerator and strategically placed the delicate gold box in the center of the table. The thudding continued up and toward the apartment door until it stopped at the top of the stairs.

With everything in place she ambled to the door and listened. There was wet breathing and a cough on the other side followed by a guttural growl that resonated as she opened the door to her brother Sam.

"Come in, we've been waiting for you, Sam." Vivian smiled. As painful as the past was, it was time for her to endure it.

Sam was bruised and soiled; his hair was tangled on top of his head. His beard was thick and straggly. He sneered at Vivian, his teeth rotted with cavities. Vivian smelled blood on his breath. At the corners of his mouth were dried stains of crimson.

"Usually on my birthday, I expect gifts, but today, I have something special for you, Sam. It's a gift that may seem familiar or maybe just a distant memory. Come in, have a seat."

Sam dragged the chair out and sat obediently. He sniffed the cupcake, his nose twitched like a rat's.

"I know you promised me that today would be the day of my death, but I fixed that, Sam. I took something from you like you took from me and I kept it. It was the only way to complete your life."

Sam stared blankly, his deep black eyes were pupil less, his stare evil and dark, his physical threat drained. Vivian poured tea in both of their cups.

"Drink up; you look like you could use a stiff drink, Sam. It must have been a journey for you in this horrible weather." Vivian giggled and sipped her tea.

"Now it's time for birthday presents." Vivian said. She took the golden box. Sam's eyes glistened. "It's a gift for me, Sam, not you. I've waited years to open this box." Vivian slowly lifted the gold hinged lid and her eyes filled with tears. She wiped them away. "It's not time for weeping. I've done enough of that; finally, it's time for joy."

Held between Vivian's thumb and index finger was a rotting severed toe. A hard, yellowing nail dangled off the end. The skin was blue and purple and a scent of decomposition wafted from the moldy interior of the once plush red lining. Vivian dangled the toe over her open mouth. Dripping saliva ran down the corners of her lips in a trail down her chin. She dropped the carrion and sucked.

Sam winced and grunted as if he felt the disappearance of the toe again. Vivian suckled for minutes until she pulled out the bone clean of flesh. Sam began to groan in pain, words tried to escape his mouth but instead rivers of blood seeped out. He shoved the chair and buckled, gimping toward the door to escape.

"Where do you think you're going?" Vivian asked. She followed him.

Sam grunted. His limp heightened and he escaped.

"You won't get far, Sam. You've been given what you always deserved but never came soon enough. Stay out of my life." Vivian shouted. She could hear the thud as he stumbled down the stairs, and the thuds grew softer.

She looked out the window at blood that trailed down the steps and into the oblivion of the snow storm,

Sam was gone, forever.

Vivian guzzled more sweet tea and opened the lid of the box. She fingered the road map on the lid one last time; felt the lining fuzzed with mold and dropped the bone into its place for safe keeping.

Vivian's life was like a box, opened now to the light, to the unhindered secrets that people whispered about her. The box gave her strength; it gave her courage, and the ability to be freed from the slavery of her past. No longer obscured by the dark hidden abuse, she locked the box away and slept a soundless slumber through the winter night. Her mind and life were one in the same, a golden trinket, velvet lined box, and macabre memories that echoed no longer were all left behind.

Shallow

Sleep; there was no better way to cope, no better way than to sleep. I slumbered in the warm ambience of the banana-yellow sun. I tuned out the world that I would someday have to wake-up and battle. Tears slipped from my eyes like leaking faucets, for what? I knew not. I turned around on my bed of soft pine needles waking slowly from much desired sleep. I had to endure the inevitability of surviving, but Death smiled a black tooth grin which spread ethereally and then chose to visit me.

Standing under the softly blowing boughs of a pine tree my back throbbed with pain, knees crackled like popcorn, and my mouth tasted coppery and bloody. I had no idea how this place came to be, how I had arrived in the shrouded dark forest only minutely lit by the sun through swaying tree branches. Home felt like planets away.

The sun's feeble rays fluttered through tree branches and the light turned gray, almost black.

Droplets of rain like tears began to fall through the trees, cascading from the leaves in tiny dribbles. I opened my mouth catching small fragments of sweet hydration.

There was a path, beaten and scarred from treks of foreign journeys ahead of me. I had to follow it, there was something foreboding in the air. I felt it bearing down on me, could feel the pressure, the pain, and even smell the rotten swampy existence of the unknown. The walk refreshed me and helped me to deduce the situation, the rain stopped and ahead on the path a clearing.

Through the shaded trail, a small river babbled. I half jogged and half ran to the source of water, the noise from the river, something other than my own thoughts and confusion, soothed me. The river rushed over large water stones worn smooth. I couldn't resist its temptation and ran to its edge. I knelt down onto the soft shoreline, scooping it into my mouth and choked. Floating atop the water, one after another, was corpses; bloated, water-logged and melted from time's endless toll and the river bed's rough terrain. I was horrified seeing the bloated bodies. They vanished in an undertow and a snapping from behind startled me back into the cold reality of the forest.

My stomach knotted like a bag of snakes, and I saw nothing. The trees swayed from a cool northern breeze and more twigs popped as if someone were coming. I knew that twigs snapping in the lonely forest could not be a good thing. There was no sign of life except for me. There were no birds, no squirrels rummaging through the forest floor for past seasons collections, not even fish jumping in the infested river or nibbling on the dead. A large blue rock stood to my right and I ducked behind it, peeking through some saplings that were sprouting up from beneath with thick wild leaves.

A bruised man appeared. He was tall, bald, with large pointy eyes; a smile spread comfortably across his jaw and disappeared up into his ears. Large rusty, red, sharpened teeth filled his smile. The man grunted, an animal grunt, an animal that I, even if I could have remembered, wouldn't be able to identify. I shuddered inside as loud bellows of laughter escaped the man. Plumes of white smoke left his mouth with each hearty chuckle.

I thought I'd seen it all, heard it all, but then the man's voice, deep and gurgling like he had just drank thick sour milk that was still caught in his throat, spoke, "I know you're there...Shallowed be Thy Name..." The man's eyes darted to and fro with a stigmatism, searching for something.

I cowered further behind the blue stone and he began to wave his hands like a magician performing some odd magic act and like a snake I slithered out into the open. He raised his arms, up and down, his fingers danced over the cool air and my eyes grew heavy, heavier, and sleep seduced me. My memories, once a distant fragment, were drawn before me. A red curtain had been lifted and the insane man somehow knew what to do to secure me with the anchors of my past.

A time of my past played. Those memories filled me with nostalgia but turned to angst because it had bothered me that I was doing nothing with my life at the time. I was accomplishing nothing, absolutely nothing. It was obnoxious that I was pulled by the weight of friendship and let the waters of life try to drown me.

Friends I had were shed quickly. My ambitions didn't have time. I needed goals to rise, see them fall. Friends were just creating an abyss, building a void of dark and drab walls in nothingness. They wanted to party, I didn't. They wanted relationships, I wasn't having it. They wanted something for nothing; I knew life was about hard work, sweat, blood and tears, to gain equity.

My empire was inspired with friendships in one way, they pushed me away and into the business world. So from the ground up, I built the Suncrest General Store in Stevats. I profited wisely by the inflation of consumables. Living in rural America, away from big city business, was the way to grab a hold of the old timer's, the worker's, the consumers of small town life in Stevats. The old blood got older, and the young blood of business thrived in a world depressed and deflated by an economy shattered like a broken window. One's loss was my gain. I lived up to my end, providing to consumers less willing to travel to spend, and they lived up to their end, spending, making me rich. No regrets, I was the king-am the king. As the memories coursed through my fogged mind I felt adrenaline yanked from me and was materialized back into the gray drab forest again. Blanketed black thunderclouds masked the sky, and the red corneas of the bruised man stared me down.

He was squatting, his haunches tight, his drawers pulled down to his knees and his face contorted. The smile that had once been eaten by the man's ears was now eaten by his neck as his lips curled into a large clowned frown. Behind the man was a massive brown turd dangling and he grunted pulling up his tattered trousers, the turd fell to the ground. He stood and if embarrassment was an emotion that the man had felt, it wasn't evident. He smiled; his pointy sharpened teeth filled the black cavity of his mouth. His long shaky index finger sported a yellow stained fingernail shook and he ambled closer.

I could smell the raw engaging stench of shit and sour milk as he said, "Shallowed be thy name." The man snickered like a smug child, his eyes soft, his lips shrouded around his pointy teeth, and he held his arms up once again.

It was an instance of magic as I fell loosely to the ground and fluttered down the path of my great life. After establishing several businesses and making money I indulged in personal gain. The finest of furniture, the finest of foods, and the finest of women, if I wanted them, I got it all. But that wasn't enough for me. I needed more; after all I was the king.

I dominated the town of Stevats and there was no one to stop me. It wasn't a curse to have ambition, it wasn't a curse to want a good life-a life of gold and treasure- it was sanity. Many people whispered about me struggling with mental break-downs because of the stress. I took medication and got better. Insanity was and always would be judged and puzzled over by the sane that is what keeps *them* sane.

My employees were paid, and while they dabbled in the lesser quality of life, I got better. They cried and struggled. I took my pills and maintained. It wasn't my fault that people let ignorance eat at them until it became a habitual style of life. They owned it; they needed to live up to the standards they set forth. Life, an endless circle of stupidity, eddied; it pulled society—so frail—into its grip and never let go. *They* let it happen themselves.

Money wasn't enough, I wanted life to be in my hands, and after several businesses flourished I opened Suncrest Nursing Home. Profit on the sick, on the poor and indigent locked away in a distant cold place on Audubon Hill. Since commodities flooded the market and people got conservative I followed suit. I downsized those commodities and ventured further into the abyss that so many business men were scared to do without the backing of a board, a committee and a bunch of rich shitty old men. When businesses plateau, I sought greater opportunities; a philosophy I had ate, slept and breathed. I did it alone popping my pills and heading down an unhealthy path that I was oblivious to.

The sick were just that, sick, and they would die; sicker people coming in to be cared for, and the nursing home was an ideal place to house those dying. It was another revolving door of cash. On only rare occasions the sick held on to their pathetic lives, as if there was something to gain by doing it, and eventually sanity's own realm would leave them an empty, hollow, shelled-out, *living* human being. They were the only speed bump with the nursing home. But I fixed that problem. I built an extension to the place on the third floor for all the crazies, the people who would not let go. And that was where they rested out their days until life's clock stopped ticking for them.

I was awakened by the smug giggles and smoke bellowing out the nostrils of the bruised man as he did a hand stand in the soft black soil and green clover. He let his legs fall and stood up, that same smile and unblinking red corneas stared at me. He grunted, grunted again, and then a large bellowing giggle escaped as if the funniest joke had been spoken.

His pointy index finger raised and his gurgling voice spoke, "Shallowed be thy name." Mr. Giggles walked closer. His rotted skin and stinky breath made me dry heave.

"Shut up, get me back home. I want to go home." I shouted. I wanted nothing more but to get back to my empire.

"Shallowed be thy name!" Mr. Giggle's voice grew louder, less gurgling, it boomed like thunder. It rattled my ears. He was larger than what distance had once given him credit. I shuddered inside, but held my ground, I wasn't going to be like those trapped in the Sunflower Room of the third floor at Suncrest Nursing Home, wasn't. I took medicine to stop the insanity. Every doctor told me to, every doctor prescribed it. I was sane?

"Get me the fuck back home." I said. It didn't dawn on me that I was asking something I had wished away. The reality of what I had just demanded was something I didn't want to face. I had run from Suncrest, I had left it behind for a reason, "I'm sorry." I whimpered but it was too late.

"Shallowed be thy name." He shouted a third time. His voice so loud that my ears rang like silver bells cascading from out of a church yard. I closed my eyes, shut the words out, shut him out, felt the dizzying spell of his madness seep into me, and consumed me. It was the third time he spoke that resulted in me vanishing from the woods. The dark forest melted around me, transforming into the void where energy floated. I was washed away, dematerialized to a truth I had been hiding from. I woke to a place created by me. But first, sleep; it was the only way to cope.

*

My ass hurt-a burning sensation on pressure points. Sunlight filtered through the large looming windows of the Sunflower Room. There were several men standing in the corner observing me with cups of pills. They rushed me and I felt defecation smearing underneath my butt. I tried to scream but words didn't come. One orderly wrapped my arms like I was a Christmas package as another threw pills into my mouth followed by a tiny cup of water holding my head back. I was forced to swallow and became dizzied. Just as my eyes began to get heavy with sleep, the seven-foot bruised man stood in the shadows of a corner. I looked at him, and in a soft whisper he spoke, *"Shallowed be thy name."*

The looming great windows of the Sunflower Room placed high above Suncrest on Audubon Hill looked out to my empire on Main Street. My stores were boarded up, folks walked by the empty shells. People sneered as they strolled by the eye sores that littered the town. The room created by my ingenuity, stress and tears loomed in sterility. The dazzling painted Sunflowers wrapped from the base of the walls up onto the ceiling and around the sky lights. The dark forest was an escape, a scary place, but in hindsight, was better than the sanitary confines of Suncrest, where nostalgia, glory and a life well spent would be dead in my world forever.

Shadeskin

A dark foreboding storm engulfed the sky and any sign of blue when Rumpelstiltskin disappeared into the ground. King Rodney and Queen Victoria Eastchill still had their daughter. Baby Jessie was spared by the victory over the manikin.

"You mustn't remember this, Jes," Queen Victoria cried swooping up Jessie, "the very devil was here but is gone forever."

"Don't talk of that tale, it's forbidden by my new law," King Rodney shook an angry finger at the Queen. He took the baby from her and left the room.

Victoria cried. Her tears were interrupted by the trembling earth, and appearance of a dark figure that shimmered into existence. There weren't hands attached to the arms just round stubbed ends. The shadow's feet floated above the ground gracefully. Bright white triangular teeth, sharpened tiny incisors, began to move as the dark blotch danced with its arms held out in the shape of a cross. The teeth chattered together, enamel clicked and tittered each time the thing opened and closed its mouth.

"Don't look, Victoria, don't look, it's the devil incarnate. It's the manikin that fooled me before, this time it's not going to work." Victoria said to herself. The shadow cornered her.

Gurgling liquid floated from the throat foaming at the thing's mouth. Words exited in thick syllables. It repeated them, slowly, but Victoria couldn't understand. She cowered in the corner shaking from fear and in silence tried to interpret what the creature was speaking. Cold air chilled the nape of her neck.

"Everyone has a wish, Victoria" the creature spoke slowly.

Victoria shuddered. "Leave me alone; I beat you, my daughter's back!"

The thing stopped swaying, and it stuttered, "I'm H-U-N-G-R-Y and you want to be free?"

Victoria could hear the cry of her baby from another chamber, "You're hungry for what?"

"I was flesh once," its voice wavered in thick liquid sound, "I need flesh off human bone." The thing formed a crooked smile of sharp incisors, spit dribbled down its chin.

Victoria raised her arm, pointed in the direction of the King's room and closed her eyes. Tears trickled in small rivers down her long cheeks. "It's him you need, that is my wish. Leave my daughter alone, and leave me alone, forever, do you promise?"

"I promise," the shade hissed and disappeared.

Terror stricken screams echoed through the castle

walls. The sound of empty promises and pleas from King Rodney didn't stop the horror that consumed him. Rodney was eaten by the creature; all that was left was bone. Baby Jessie was lying on the cold cement floor. Victoria scooped her into her arms and abandoned the life that she had regretted since its evil beginning from miller to royalty.

Evil flesh formed again, Rumpel-stiltskin lived. The castle of King and Queen Eastchill was desolate, but not empty. A harsh, large mass of cloud infested the sky and engulfed the castle-tittering-laughter and terror echoed within.

Melancholy

Jack Sprout was pissed, his face cherry red. He strode down Flagitious Street fast and angry, leaving his home behind him on Maple and Fifth in the dust. Jack was heading towards a house that sat on the dead end of Flagitious, a drab gray Victorian. His grandparents had died three years ago. It was empty except for distant memories that lingered like lost energy. Jack had to get away from his kids, from his wife, from the demons that stormed like evil mercenaries, hidden in the obscurity of his past and in his mind.

Before becoming pissed-off, Jack made pancakes for breakfast, flipped on cartoons for the kids in the front room and served his wife in bed. He had sex with Janet while the kids were occupied, it was a rare moment when Janet's psychotic personality hadn't flared and picked at Jack for something he didn't do. Afterward something, maybe the subliminal snide comments coming from Janet in the background noise, snapped inside. Jack couldn't stop a flare of words, actions, and—*melancholy*—flooded him.

Jack's head spun like a tightly wound top and he pumped his arms back and forth power walking. He stopped for seconds to light a cigarette, inhaled deeply, and continued onward. Jack puffed on the smoke, blew it out, and rid himself of the explosion that occurred at home. He needed peace; needed quiet and the gray faded Victorian would do the trick. He didn't know how his grandparent's old home would sooth him, wisp away the pain, but there was *something* in the ethereal sidelines telling him all would be okay if he were to pay a visit to the vacant place. Jack flicked the cigarette on the street, a gust of wind picked it up and shuttled it into a plush green yard of a nearby house.

Most of the houses were empty with for sale signs swinging on the front yards of Flagitious Street. Jack and his family had all refused to sell his grandparents' house. The yard was overgrown with weeds and old, worn paint flaked off on the wood siding; it had been out of sight and out of mind.

Jack remembered Sunday mornings. His grandparents used to swing on the front porch in their later years, incapable of doing anything except their old age routine and Jack would often come and take them to church. They would wait for him and then stroll through the quiet bedroom community. It was the least that Jack could do for them. Chills ran through as the memory faded like a ghost caught dancing on his grave, but he didn't believe in ghosts. Jack quickly jumped up the porch steps. He lifted his fist to knock and realized he was sucked in the past and that there was no one home.

In the distance St. Stephen's church bells rang a sad requiem that floated through the air like lost yesteryears.

"Damn it," Jack sniffled, tears filled his eyes. The elegy reminded Jack of his grandparents. His hands shook as he stuffed one into his pocket to get the keys. He wiped away a stream of snot that had ventured down his upper lip and a flow of tears that rolled down his face. He felt like a damned child.

The glum-raged rhetoric and physicality of the early afternoon was violent, but Jack was already forgetting. Maybe by visiting his grandparent's empty house he could recollect how to be a good person, husband and dad. His grandparents were always good to him when they raised him, so there would have to be some answers that would sooth the unanswered questions burning inside.

The door swung open, singing rusty songs of nostalgia. In the living room the furniture had a fine layer of dust over most of it, making it look like an untouched tomb. Jack stepped over the threshold and shut the door behind him. Already he was at ease. His grandparent's had raised him from a very young age and he was grateful of the good memories of his childhood. He never remembered what happened to his parents or much about them. He recognized his grandparent's as the only parental figures in his life. He never questioned their intentions. It was what it was and he turned out a good man because they had raised him well, *God?* rest their souls. He made the sign of the cross not realizing it had been upside down.

Old habits die hard.

Standing in the living room of his youth helped to

sweep the flawed afternoon with his family under the proverbial carpet. Jack sat down on the loveseat. Dust floated into the air and settled like un-melted snowflakes to the wood floors. He took in a deep breath, wanted a cigarette, but knew his grandparents didn't allow smoking in their house. A *thump* from upstairs, loud and out of line, startled Jack.

"Who's here?" His voice was muffled by the clutter of the dark paneled walls. Built in book cases and shelving units lined the walls from floor to ceiling with Hummel's and trinkets filling empty space.

Thump, this time the noise was louder and followed by a low growl. Jack felt his bowels churn and a cold chill in the air. The tiny hairs on his neck stood on end, his breath exited in plumes of white smoke. His flesh crawled with goosebumps.

"Who's here?" Jack asked again. There was no answer and the noises stopped.

It's just me, you remember, don't you Jack?

Jack was startled at the words; terror flitted through his flesh like high voltage.

He was near frozen on the loveseat but stood up hoping that he didn't shit himself. A strong urge to run out the front door passed as he listened for more. The bathroom was around the corner by the kitchen. It was tucked under the servant's staircase. Jack calmed himself by rubbing together his frozen hands. He had to get to the bathroom. He could feel his bowels move closer to their exit and slowly pinched the muscles from retracting.

The grumble became louder, deeper.

Jack ran, his muscles loosened, sweat layered his

arms and face. Horrific scenes of gore ran like film strips through Jack's head. Memories of his wife and kids stung like stigmata but the terror at hand allowed them to burrow deeply away and helped him forget. Jack bolted for the bathroom.

The toilet was cold and Jack was relieved that he made it. Sitting in the tight quarters was claustrophobic and he counted. This was something Jack did when he was nervous, counted to ten, took deep breaths, with his eyes closed, and he gained control of many situations doing it. He inhaled deeply, exhaled, and counted each breath. By the tenth time the house rattled underneath, the old tiles of the bathroom lifted and fell back into place. The cupboards in the kitchen swooshed open and slammed shut. Jack slowly opened his eyes and it all stopped.

Jack wanted to run to the living room and bolt out of the house. He couldn't. He wasn't a quitter. There was something he had to do in the old place before he left it. Silence was thick, but underneath it all Jack knew the cellar is where the answers were.

Moonlight washed through the tall leaded window in the kitchen. The sky was clear and starry, a backdrop of perfect night. Jack had barely seconds to admire it when the cellar door creaked open and an illuminating rose colored light flooded the cool kitchen tile. Fear was rampant and adrenaline pumped in proportion to his heart beat. Flee, fight, quit. Jack did none.

Scents of earth and mustiness rose from the depths of the old Michigan basement. Jack took one step slowly descending the worn wooden staircase. Unknown words languidly floated on top of all other sounds. Jack plugged his ears as they metamorphosed into incantations of another tongue. The steady mantras lead him down into the cellar. There was a large square cistern in the floor where light scattered in illuminating throes.

The sounds were louder from the cistern. Jack was chilled to the bone, shivering uncontrollably as something wet slithered upward from the dank hole. Two brackish things with large fleshy bulbs at the ends peered through the ambient light and glared at Jack. The bulbs were red with rivers of veins crawling like roads over the spheres. Jack tried to move his feet, tried to run, but instead shuffled away from the cistern.

A muscular, bipedal creature clambered the rest of the way from the reservoir and ambled towards Jack. Beads of water on black smooth skin and deep-set yellow eyes terrorized. The things that had peeked at Jack were stiff, curved horns with round meaty ends that resembled eyes but were fleshy bulbs. The lips of its mouth were pierced together and turned upward in a smile exposing sharp black incisors that hung over the bottom lip. Jack stifled a scream. The monstrous oddity shuffled closer. Low guttural growls on the surface morphed into whispers which changed to speech within seconds of leaving the creatures mouth.

"You've done well, Jack. You've held up to your end of the deal." The demon schlepped closer.

"What the fuck are you talking about?" Jack trembled.

"No need for vulgarity, you've been chosen; you've accomplished your sacrifice. Now I must pay you for it." The creature stopped. Its eyes furrowed into narrow slits.

If it weren't for the unfurling smile on the monster's face Jack would think it was angry.

"Okay, can I go, since I've held up to my end of the deal?" Jack asked. His memory slowly seeped back, slowly revealing what he had been running from.

"Follow me." It said to Jack.

On the creature's back were fleshy faces, unfamiliar and shrouded with the obscured dark of the unlit basement. It walked and Jack followed. Black swallowed them both. Yellow light of the creature's eyes was the only thing breaking the gloom and illuminated a pentagram drawn on the floor.

Jack's heart pounded in the chest and his head began to pound. The demon stared blankly; his black teeth chattered together with fervor. The events of that afternoon unfolded, by hypnosis, shadows of a dark scene, and Jack was dulled, his mind spun uncontrollably.

"You killed her, Jack. Your wife, your sacrifice," the demon said.

Jack's stomach was a knotted mess. His head hurt and a flood of uncharacterized evil spilled itself in spinning memory:

Flashes of hot sex, Janet was nude, spread for him, waiting. Jack stood with a knife, clean, sharp and new. Jack swung the knife; it swooshed through the air, Janet's head lopped off like a dandelion. He was surprised at how clean and fast the process was. Janet landed with a thud, bright red blood stained the bedroom floor, Looney Tunes theme music played from the living room television downstairs. Jack remembered thinking that it would be far more difficult to do such a thing with the spinal cord in the back of her neck, but it wasn't.

Momma had a baby and her head popped off!

Jack's memory switched to the demon's growling voice, "Your grandparent's did it to your parents. You sacrificed your wife. The family wheel of dark service keeps turning."

"I didn't, I couldn't have..." Jack stammered.

"You did," The demon moved close.

Jack cried. His head hurt worse and pounded like a tom-tom with every beat of his heart. He made the inverted sign of the cross.

Old habits die hard.

He was taught the sign at age twelve at service and probably buried it along with everything else he wished he could forget. It was all seeping back. Jack searched for something, something to wash it all away. He needed the realization that maybe he had just hallucinated the murder/sacrifice of Janet. It was a nightmare, a floating, obscene vision of terror.

"You're doing just fine, Jack. Let me give you this, it's your turn to write in it. I will leave. It's yours now." The demon walked forward. The smell of rotten fish, earth, and stagnant water were pungent, "It's the last step in your journey back to life in Stevats."

The monstrosity handed Jack an old book bound in yellow rotted flesh. The flesh was made of a dried animal skin. Fragments of grey/brown fur still clung to the dried caked tissue. On the front of the book was an inverted cross and a red Albatross. Jack's hands trembled.

"What do I write?" Faintly the church bells requiem

faded into oblivion outside.

"You write your wife's Stencil Ceremony. You get your family back. The Ceremony will be read by someone else."

"What, where, who?"

"The negative side of your wife's life, the dirt, the scoop, the nitty-gritty details, the shit stains, they're the only things I or anyone else truly care about. Only then will your family be given back to you." The demon walked back to the cistern.

Jack pulled out an old pencil and wrote feverishly. Sweat bubbled on his face, dripped in salty rivers down his mouth and chin as he finalized the page. He stood on shaky legs, ambled to the center of the pentagram and threw the book.

He curled into the fetal position on the dank floor. Sleep was the only way to cope and it came easily. His head was invaded by nightmares and days of recovery as he slipped in and out of unconsciousness, his mind purging the horrible recollections. On the sixth day, Jack was welcomed by light; he was in the master bedroom of his house on the corner of Fifth and Maple Street. A cross of St. Stephen's steeple glimmered in the eastern sun through the window.

The house, the demon, the book was a fragment, just a crumb in his mind. A familiar ***thump***, echoed from downstairs. The smell of rotted fish, stagnant water and a whispering incantation filled the stairwell.

This can't be real. Jack thought. Tears dangled in the corners of his eyes. He prayed, made the sign of an inverted cross.

Old habits never die.

The ***thump*** was louder. Jack's bowels churned. He counted to ten, taking deep breaths. The bedroom door creaked open. Languidly floating on the top of background noise was a steady mantra, familiar and constant. Janet walked through the door.

"Ready for breakfast," she asked.

She moved a strand of hair from Jack's eyes.

Sharp black incisors rested on her bottom lip and on the top of her head two small horns curved forward. Jack's eyes were large wide saucers, and a dark fanatical smile filled his face. He followed Janet downstairs and they were greeted by the familiar background noise of Saturday morning cartoons.

Jargon

The dread, the terror fell before dawn. Red rivers of blood stuck to the bark of trees—sinewy chunks rolled down the streams of crimson. Shane was awake, alone, and didn't quite remember how the night's events played out or how he had survived. It had been an onslaught. A rage filled night when the sun brightly hued in the west sinking to its demise and the moon replaced its bright yellow glow. Terror unleashed then at that moment.

A grunt brought Shane back, deep, guttural and coming from the trees behind him.

"Unk-Unk," the indecipherable noise started.

What the fuck is that? Shane thought. He grew more fearful, more alert, but still scared of the horror that lurked behind him.

"Unk-Unk," The grunt repeated.

Shane's stomach turned, jumped, floated like a butterfly and his heart raced. Shane hoped for relief, but as he tried to push the flooding memories of last night aside they continued to surface like the tide, washing into his mind violently.

Shane wanted to be home, needed to be safe, he had to survive the pulverization that had happened to everyone at the party, had to escape death. The low hanging branches of the woods welted his face as last night revisited.

*

It started out innocently, as every party did. This time, no one went home, they died at the hands of the deranged man. Booze had been flowing, everyone laughing, red faced and slurring words when Jerry, a courier, stood in the front door. The moon glowed behind him, a bright white backdrop of satin, and his eyes shone a funny red.

Mike, who worked with Shane, staggered toward Jerry. Jerry wore a grin that exposed all of his butter yellow teeth in a sneer. He lurched toward Mike and smashed his head. Mike's body fell limply to the floor with a thud. The remnants of Mike's head looked like a smashed mural of tomato paste sticking to the walls. There were other's from the lab who started puking, others wretched over like they were inflicted with decompression sickness—holding hands over their mouths, cheeks full of vomit—and Shane ran upstairs. The screams were unbearable and when what sounded like a stampede exited the front door, he felt safe enough to move and ran from the house into the woods.

Shane was greeted by a dark web of grotesque blood and guts surrounding him as well as the grunts from the deranged specimen courier. Shane couldn't imagine what the unbalanced Jerry had in mind or what he was trying to say, but knew that it was life or death. Fight or flight. The realization that there were no survivors hit home and a maze of horror movies flashed through Shane as he saw the glimmering soft glow of home through the bordering property line of pine trees. He wanted more than anything to get back there, had wished he never left in the first place.

"Unk-Unk," Terror chilled Shane.

Was home safe, or home a trap at this point? As always, his home is where the heart was, at least the heart of several co-workers, and Shane took off towards it in a sprint.

Stumbling into the front door the smell of blood was pungent. Shane's eyes grew watery. He ran upstairs for safety and bolted into his bedroom. For a master suite, it was the smallest room in the three-bedroom house, but it felt the safest place to be. In one corner was a Thin Prep 2000, only a non working prop, just like the one at work where he processed Thin Prep specimens from gynecologist offices. Shane liked something at home to remind him of work. He flipped the lights out and cowered close to the cardboard prop, stifling a nervous laugh.

*

It had started at work. It was the Thin Prep 2000 machine. At work Shane was a lab tech and processed Thin Prep containers. These were small plastic cylinders that gynecologists collected cervical samples in and used the solution to contain the specimen. The specimen, with container, was placed on the Thin Prep machine and it worked its magic, whizzing, and buzzing-voila, the cervical specimen was stamped neatly on a slide in a full moon circle for the technologists to screen.

The process after the slides is what stirred Shane's quirky sense of boredom and routine; he felt deserving of such humor because he had become the Thin Prep King, processing over two hundred of the dreaded slides in an eight-hour shift, more than triple the amount of slides the other orangutan techs did. The cylinders had to be categorized and placed in sequence to process in a stock room, so follow up referencing could be done by the technologists if requested.

Shane in the darkly lit room, while organizing and categorizing, said to his boss that these specimens are being stocked in the back of the lab. They should be called Backstock! Shane's boss loved the idea. Shane used the word "backstock" so fluently that people began to think he went mad, until they jumped right in and began speaking the same language. Jerry, the courier, was enraged by the backstock pandemic. Jerry despised Shane's good sense of humor and likeability.

Shane had been in the back-room, backstocking, and Jerry was walking by. Shane hummed a tune, "I— want to *baaackstock* all night, and backstock everyday…"

"Do you have to say that damn word all the time? You're driving me nuts!" Jerry's eyes angered his brows thick and twisted like fury night crawlers. Shane was scared and since his co-workers had been having so much fun with it, it was majority rule—the word was going nowhere. Jerry towered at six foot six and had an enlarged forehead. His eyes were separated too far apart indicating there may have been fetal alcohol poisoning and his gene pool pissed in one too many times.

"Well, it's part of my job, I love backstock!" Shane shouted and danced a jig.

"I love my fiancé, but I don't go around singing her name and saying her name all the time." Jerry said. He left Shane mumbling angrily and stomping like a small child.

As time passed, jobs at Stevats' Memorial Laboratory, as well as everywhere else, started to merge and "globalize" (it was a corporate way of putting people into jobs to get things done without hiring). Shane adapted well to jobs added to his workload, embraced the idea, but couriers, they were a different breed of people, especially the loose canon Jerry. Jerry had been infuriated at the news of having to backstock and "globalize". Shane walked by everyday just to mention the word backstock. Jerry disappeared, stayed calm and Shane felt that he finally converted or just learned to ignore everyone else and the lab's humor.

Shane had to say it as he passed the room and opened his mouth to speak. Warm chunks of puke filled his speechless mouth. Jerry stood on a ladder, a thick clear chunky liquid slipping down his chin and a Thin Prep bottle to his lips (got milk?). He was drinking the backstock. Shane decided rather than saying anything to his supervisor, he would just leave work early and get ready to party the night away, drink the horror of Jerry's biohazard fetish away.

That night, and in an inebriated stupor, Shane was cracking jokes about the specimen monster. He explained the mythos further and indicated that it was a specimen thief that ran rampant through the lab drinking biohazard material and stealing everyone's backstock.

Everyone guessed that Shane was cracking jokes about Jerry, but Shane, even though drunk to the point of incoherence, knew that he spoke the truth. Everyone got a good chuckle out of it until they were pulverized by ungodly strength and shouted at with indecipherable jargon.

*

Shane coward in the corner of his room, sober, and grasping what he had to face in the present. He heard the front door creak open. His gut churned and a small glimmering metal needle caught his eye. Although the Thin Prep prop was cardboard, its authenticity did have some attributes that were genuine. There was a sharp needle that simulated the original needle used to grab the specimen through a rubber seal and mix it with solution. Shane grabbed it. It was large enough for a weapon. He stood behind his bedroom door and waited, his bowels churned like sickly snakes.

One by one the old wooden stairs of the house creaked and heavy, wet breathing of a monster walked whispering, "Unk-Unk."

The gibberish filled the hallway and grew closer. Shane feared the worst, his hands trembled. The master bedroom door opened slowly, faint yellow light spread over darkness. Shane waited, scared shitless.

The door opened half way and Jerry's tall shadow cast itself on the rectangle display of light on the floor. Shane jumped at him with all the force he could strum up and plunged the needle into Jerry's neck. Jerry's large hands went to his neck and Shane drew the needle out quickly moving away. Most people when stabbed in the neck with a needle would have bled, Shane expected a geyser of blood to stream, to paint a macabre picture on the walls, but a small trickle of clear liquid seeped out in a thick viscous pus.

Shane backed toward the bay window. Sunflower Street looked too far away and too far down. A street light flickered off as the sun started rising in the east. Shane wanted to be cutting grass, taking a nap, going to work, anything other than dealing with this creep who made drinking backstock a living.

Jerry bolted forward, a slow moving freight train, a Mack truck in first gear all but a blur of speed and agility. Shane held the needle firm and as Jerry went for the neck he rammed the needle into the deranged man's chest. Jerry let out an animal grunt and his hands loosened. Shane leapt into the air, turned and kicked Jerry with all the strength his tired legs could muster. The monster lost balance and shattered the glass of the large bay window, falling out the second story. Shane heard Jerry shouting something, something that would both haunt and cure anymore wisecracks or obnoxiousness at work. He heard him screaming, "BACKSTOCK!"

*

It had been a nightmare, all of it, the party, the made up nonsense word of the day, the entire explanation to the cops, the forensics who were investigating Jerry's body, but in the end, Shane was thankful for his own life. There was a non-denominational service held for the victims paid for by Stevats' Memorial Hospital at St. Peter's Church and Shane attended. He felt responsible for the entire incident although the authorities cleared him of any wrong doing. Grief stricken and sad he sat near the back of the church in a pew closest to the door for an easy escape to avoid any inquiring, nosy Stobbits (the small minded citizens of Stevats as Shane referred to them). Before the service ended Shane bolted out, and when the bright sunlight of day warmed his face the shrubs to his left moved shaking, rattling, coming to life. Shane turned, and as gooseflesh crawled up his arms tried to rationalize that it must have been a breeze, had to be. As he began to walk away jargon filled his ears, "Unk-Unk." Words of nightmares revisited him.

Shane ran fast, doubting that speed would ever get him to safety...

Blood Flower

Moonlit walks, carriage rides and the local saloon were all attributes within the village of Stevats. Confined in that history, deep inside the core were lies, sin, and punish-ment. The punishment of accountability always ended on Sunflower Row.

Before the lane had become street, before it was paved, and lined with homes nestled in a tightly knit neighborhood, Sunflower Street was a death sentence. Planted on both sides of the foot-path were acres of vast radiant sunflowers that lilted on cloudy days and tilted upwards on sunny days. Sunflower Row, the path, was a bruised trail that led to an old sprawling oak tree. It was a channel designed specifically for criminals to walk death's lingering stretch to the hangman's noose for execution. Stevats was an arcane society in its beliefs.

It was on Sunday that the Death Walk would come for those to be executed. Sunday's were days of church, family luncheons and at twelve noon a spot along

Sunflower Row. Waiting in line to pay with his death was Jake Heathcowski. His stomach crawled with anxiety; it felt like a bag of angry snakes that writhed like mad creatures trying to make an exit. Sheriff Daniels arrested Jake for purportedly raping a grieving widow.

Widow Schmitz was at her husband's grave and Jake Heathcowski allegedly took advantage of her sullen demure. It was said that he bent the widow over her husband's gravestone and violently sodomized her. The attack was seen by a small seven-year-old playing in a sandbox in his back yard. The boy reported it to his mom, who then reported it to Sheriff Daniels. Jake Heathcowski was apprehended and arrested for the crime and sentenced to hang.

His parents, two illiterate Polish immigrants, could barely comprehend the English ways and American life, let alone teach their son, so Jake grew up learning life from peers and the cold arms of school and neighbors. Jake never hated his parents for it. He understood their struggles as immigrants and their indifferences to the world around them. He blamed no one for the society of ignorance that often shunned him and his family.

Jake stood in shackles at the entrance of Sunflower Row. He shivered inside. Despite the humidity, despite the lemon yellow sun glowing overhead, a cold crisp winter chill froze the marrow in his bones. The day was melancholic. It crept slowly and gave Jake an opportunity to reflect on the past, on the present and of the future awaiting him. If he was going to meet his maker he needed to clear his conscious.

The early birds set up their seats along the path in

the center of the two fields of sunflowers. The first people to arrive made a morning event out of the hanging; these were the non-church goers. This group was sullen and their faces were drawn. Not the typical crowd of people who showed up for an execution. The true spectators wouldn't arrive until church let out.

Jake's chill grew deeper. It was a bit ironic that the people who had no faith in God would show up with more sympathy than the Christians. It was also a blatant hypocrisy of the way the world was. Jake tried to smile at the early arrivals and they quickly turned from him. He could see their sad eyes turned sympathetic and could sense the awkward movements as they autonomously set up their seats along the trail. These people weren't there to be entertained; they were there only to bear witness to the atrocity against their fellow man. One by one they each pulled journals out of satchels recording the climate, the time, the date and the detail. They took their roles in death and retribution seriously.

Growing over the distant sky line and shadowing the hanging tree, Jake could see the Church's steeple stretched above a cupola in town. It rose upward and the polished copper glistened in the morning sunlight. Jake squinted at the sun. The ringing Church bell taunted him in melodious requiem as the music, in a harsh tintinnabulation, called the parishioners to worship. The bells mocked Jake's life, they were alive and within the next four hours he would be gasping for air, clinging for his life as he was hanged. It was a bizarre celebration of the end of Jake's life. It was written in Stevats' law that he would have to wait from eight in the morning until noon before taking the walk down Sunflower Row.

Jake wanted to shout his innocence.

There was no remorse. There wasn't the least bit of sympathy for the widow. The only emotion surging through Jake was the terror of death. The hanging tree creaking from a northerly breeze taunting his every nerve. It was fear and death that woke the macabre dark memory of that day which unfolded the path of his demise.

*

The recollections were gray and drab. Jake never visited his parents' graves before, but on the day of the incident with the widow he wanted to pay his respects and enjoy the sunshine. His parents had been dead for years and Jake disconnected from them both emotionally and on a level he had never believed himself capable.

Black clouds covered the sunshine, dark and unmoving, casting forlorn shadows through the cemetery. It was safe for Jake to assume there would be nobody at the graveyard to spot him. Jake was a wanderer, a person who had no one, people despised him because he didn't go to church and didn't get involved, he was awkward around them and they had always judged him for that. The only positive thing that lined the cold grave stones was flowers placed in front of them by others that had visited. People respected the dead more than they did the living. Jake found his parents' burial and knelt in front of the small tribute. He wasn't a prayerful person but thought to himself about the past and how his parents had struggled in a foreign land to raise him. Tears formed in his eyes like pools of still water.

A loud black bird screeched from a nearby old growth tree and startled Jake. He remembered hunting with his father and his father endlessly complaining that the black birds were warning deer and small game of their demise. Jake shivered at the haunting voice of his father. He shivered the resonating voice away and was taken to a small dark patch of woods, dimly lit by a flower.

In the dim overcast, swallowed by the overpowering shadows, was an illuminated yellow sunflower. The unmistaken beauty put Jake in a trance; he stumbled trying to gain his balance over fallen twigs and tree brush until he reached the wanton place of the early bloom.

The flower's petals weren't like other sunflowers. At the tips of each petal was a bright crimson circle, like an artist had dripped red paint on them. Jake picked it, broke the stem off the bottom and put it in his jacket. A strong lavender perfume drifted over the compost scents left from winter and Jake was taken back by a princess dressed in black.

She was smooth-skinned and supple; her bosom large and her hourglass shape designed for eye candy, Jake got an erection. He ambled forward. The young widow, her face laced with a black veil, spotted him and stood up. A look of surprise and bewilderment, wild, like an animal's, filled her eyes. Jake wanted nothing but to hear her voice. He imagined it sounded as sweet as an angel's.

The woman trembled as Jake walked closer. Her trembling turned into convulsions and she fell to the ground, her body shook uncontrollably. Her tongue lolled out the side of her mouth and Jake acted. He sat her up, her bright green eyes rolled into the back of her head. He propped her onto the headstone, her convulsions grew worse. Her condition was bizarre, something Jake had never seen. He turned her over the headstone and her body lay motionless and stiff under his own. Stressed and sweating he slid off and down to the ground for a rest.

The princess breathed heavily, her breath raspy and wet. Jake thought that she was going to convulse again and so he fled. More than a little socially awkward Jake feared that remaining here would only make things worse for him. He couldn't believe that he saved her from her first bought of convulsions.

The trees, the tombstones and the dark shadows of an overcast sky blurred as he ran home. His lungs burned, his eyes were weary and heavy, and he fell into his soft bed, instantly trying to purge the day. He hoped he did the right thing. A pounding on his door jolted him from sleep and he was arrested and charged with rape, a crime punishable by death.

*

The memory faded slowly, the crime Jake faced punishment for, lingered inside. He wanted to tell the truth, but no one would listen to him, it was too late. The sun slowly crept higher and closer to noon. The large copper cross that rested on top of the church's steeple began to shadow the tops of the trees. A rash broke out on his hands and feet and Jake grimaced, his mouth forming an odd, insane smile. Someone, mistaking his grimace for laughter, punched him in the side. It was one of the guards. Jake buckled at the blow and stood up holding the spot where he was pounded. The guard sneered at him, his teeth yellow and clenched, and his eyes two slits of anger. He could almost hear the guard hissing like a snake but knew it was imagination. He knew that his end was near and that there was nothing in the world that could save his life.

With so much to gain by living, Jake made promises to whoever was listening in the cosmos, that ethereal world that he never truly believed in until now when he needed it the most. He swore that he'd never be bad, would always do the right thing, follow the right path, and then he remembered the flower he found in the cemetery.

It was alone, sheltered by the shaded area of trees in the border. It was growing where no other sunflower did and survived. In hindsight Jake realized the flower was like him in many aspects. The blemished sunflower in his pocket meant something, but what? His panicked mind raced for an answer and suddenly he heard his mother whisper, *Krew kwiatów.* He shivered and thought of the story his mother told him as a boy, what little he did learn of the Polish language the words meant, *Blood Flower.*

"Luck it brings to those who hold it, Jake, luck and nothing else. It rests alone in many sacred places, long before humans, many years before this tarnish." His mother used to tell him. She would wave her hands flutteringly emphasizing the tarnish of all material things and what evils lurked within people. *"You must never underestimate the sacred trust of nature, and what blessings they deliver, never."*

Jake, from the lost memory, felt some relief

remembering the story. But it wasn't enough reassurance to comfort him in the time of death and his walk down Sunflower Row. He wished to look at the dormant flower in his pocket, maybe it was a charm, a talisman that would bring luck to him, for all he knew it was a Blood Flower. He longed for another glimpse of his past, maybe a time when his mother described the flower. He couldn't, his mind was exhausted, his body ached from standing and the discomforts continued.

Jake took in a deep breath and when the guards looked away he fumbled for the sunflower in his pocket. He was able to get one hand in; the cold hard steel of the cuffs prevented him from pushing in deeper. His meditation had been on such a deep level that he didn't realize that it was fifteen minutes from high noon, and the Death Walk.

Carriages of church goers dressed in their Sunday's best lined the side of the old trail, leaving just enough room for Jake to walk down. He could hear children playing and chasing after one another, he heard the religious folks murmur amongst one another. It was a slow progression at first and turned into a loud outpouring of chatter. Jake's stomach flipped, flopped, and a small dose of vomit filled the back of his throat. It burned and it took all he could muster to force it back down.

Short bursts of acidic bile continued stinging his tonsils and his tongue. Jake was overpowered by the urge to puke as the two guards began to manhandle him. *The sunflower didn't work.* He thought. He almost tripped on a rough patch of the trail and regained his balance.

The executioner waited under the oak tree at the end of Sunflower Row. He was dressed in brown leather from head to toe, a wide tooth grin spread beneath his leather mask. The sight of the man who would place the noose around Jake's neck and kick the bucket from underneath him was terrifying. The man showed no remorse, only raw humor in the act he was about to perform.

The sun was brazen and Jake's armpits were drenched with sweat. His lips were dry and his throat parched. Halfway down death's trail he saw a small red drop fall from the sky. It was followed by another, and another until a full torrential downpour of a thick viscous liquid showered everyone. Jake thought it was rain and stuck out his tongue; it tasted of copper and salt. Sinewy chunks of the gelatinous substance landed over the crowd. The spectators bunched their children together, trying to block the falling substance. They herded like lost sheep. Jake wanted to laugh but the true slaughter began before he could blink.

The sunflowers in the field waved and wisped by a faint breach of air, each of the petals were painted with drops of red that fell from the sky, a mirror image to the flower in Jake's pocket. The executioner stood unflinching because he had a job to do and the guards that were once watching him vanished. Jake searched for his captors, hoping that they had left him to his own devices, and on the ground beneath each guard's clothing was a mound of waxy tissue. Four bloody eyeballs stared up at him from the ground as if pleading for help. A burning sensation rose in the back of Jake's throat and this time he couldn't stifle the vomit, he let it go.

People fled from the horror show of others melting away to nothing but lumps of skin and blood. They screamed as each person vanished like ice cubes on a hot day. Their flesh stretched, shrank and the meaty tissue beneath their skin melted.

Jake wondered why the executioner wasn't gone from the acidic down pour. It was the brown leather, somehow it protected him. He wanted to yell at the man but instead fell to the ground. Although untouched and unscathed by the pouring of crimson, everyone turned into unrecognizable monstrosities, and the fact that the executioner still stood was a miracle, *Krew kwiatów,* Jake shivered at the haunting words of his mother and saw the glimmer of keys lying by the guard's mound of flesh. He bent; kept his eyes on the man in leather for any moves he may have in store, and picked them up.

There were two keys on the ring and only one that unlocked the cuffs that wrapped his wrists. The first key worked, Jake's hands were free. He unlocked the shackles around his ankles, the ground trembled, and then stillness. The leather man left his post. Jake could almost see the piercing green eyes through the openings of the leather shroud covering his face.

"Hold it right there, Jake Heathcowski, by the power invested in me by the village of Stevats, I must," the voice was loud and belonged to Sheriff Daniels, "make you pay for the crimes you committed!"

The Sheriff walked through slush piles of sinewy leftovers, his head high, his gait slow and confident. Jake wanted to bolt through the patches of sunflowers. He wanted to get away from Sunflower Row, from the stench of melted carrion, and as far away from Stevats as he could, but something stopped him, it was the presence of something more evil, but was saving his life. He looked at the flower which he held in a fist and blood dripped from it.

Jake opened his hand and the sunflower was crumpled, its yellow petals milky and red, the dots had saturated each petal reaching the center, brackish liquid ran into his palm down his wrist. Jake's flesh crawled with goosebumps.

Shaky words left his dry mouth, "Coward!" Although Jake shouted, the word was soft. The executioner stopped.

Beads of sweat trickled from out of the Sheriff's mask and down the eye holes, and he answered, "I don't think I heard you right." The Sheriff laughed, his laugh was shrill and pitched with authority.

"You, Sheriff, you're hiding behind a mask. I'm here in the open walking to my death and you don't want me to see your face. That's a coward." Saliva rejuvenated Jake's mouth.

"You're the one who must pay with your life, Jake Heathcowski."

"I want to see your face. If I don't then I won't agree to your sentence. I was falsely accused." Jake said. A sense of relief filled him. Jake ambled closer to the sweating executioner.

Sheriff Daniels paused. The sun beat down on the path stiffening the air. Jake hoped he was getting through just enough for the Sheriff to lose attention on what was happening.

The Sheriff chuckled, "I can't hear you."

"There's nothing shackling me, there are no guards to apprehend me, I'm as free as you, Sheriff." Jake said.

He reluctantly grabbed his mask. Jake's stomach writhed with apprehension; he knew he was going to make a run for it.

"No matter what happens, Jake Heathcowski, you're a dead man." He pulled the leather hood off.

The summer heat rose to noxious desert warmth, and more red splotches fell. The sunflowers waved in a welcomed dance as each was doused with yet another dot of red on top of the previous blemish. The Sheriff's eyes bulged out of his forehead. His tongue, swollen and red, plopped out of his mouth landing on the ground with a thud. His large calloused hands grabbed his throat as he wheezed for air. Like a wax candle made of flesh his face began to fall off. Blood and other bodily fluids swirled in a downward spiral and into the mound of flesh.

A cool northerly breeze blew. The hanging tree creaked and groaned, all had disappeared. A faint ringing of what was left of the church bells requiem vanquished into the breeze and Jake stumbled forward. Befuddled and confused he looked down at the fluidity of melted tissue that was once Sheriff Daniels. An old familiar voice, his mother's, in her broken polish dialect, whispered two words that assured Jake that all was well and life would go on: *Krew kwiatów*.

Jake whistled and strolled away from Sunflower Row. The Blood Flower a memory, a whispered tale from his mother who wanted to warn him about the way things were. Jake relished the memory, stored it inside and left everything behind.

35

1

Lurking beneath the floorboards was something creeping, seething within the dirt under the house. It was invisible, but would scratch at the floor joists and growl, very low, very deep and menacing. The trailer walls were thin, the floor joists metal, so each clawed scratch sounded like nails to a chalkboard. Alyssa shuddered, burrowing herself beneath the blanket that was flowered with unicorns, the only form of security in a world of insecurities. A storm cell had drifted into Stevats, had been drifting in for a day or two, and a black cover obscured the very stars and moon that gave night time its only light. Alyssa peaked through a hole in the blanket, and lightening lit the sky and she shook.

She could hear her dad coughing. It seemed like he was a mile away, and she knew that he wouldn't do anything for her. He was passed-out on his chair; had been for a couple hours. Her mother died when Alyssa was three, she barely knew her. She had often wondered when the creatures under the trailer first began to surface in her life and realized that they started around the time her father became a drunk, after mom died.

Alyssa's dad, Edmond, played the victim, constantly throwing a poor pity party and the bottle was helping him celebrate. Edmond was a laborer and worked at Briber Plastics. When Elizabeth died of rabies, Edmond took to the bottle, lost his job and slowly declined. He liked his buddy Jack Daniels the most, but would settle for anything with alcohol in it.

The scratching stopped for a spell. Alyssa wondered if the monstrosity that lurked beneath the floor boards was just as scared about the storm as she was of *it*. If *it* was just as scared, Alyssa hoped the storm would carry on for as long as it could because that meant some sanity for her and finally some sleep.

Her father's binges kept her awake. She remembered the first time she witnessed one of his stupors. She got home from school and he was mumbling, passed out on the recliner. His eyes were squinted and his facial stubble, which he usually kept shaved and trimmed, was like wild bush. His teeth were yellow and Alyssa never saw him so ugly and unkempt. He was, in her young eyes, changing, morphing into something that no one really wanted to see.

She cooked them both macaroni and cheese that night, he had been barely able to feed himself. Each forkful would fall off because Alyssa made it too milky and she ended up feeding him with a spoon. He slurped each bite down. She saw the life coming back, or enough life that he could stand on his own and stumbled to the bathroom. He peed and fell to floor in the hallway. She helped him the best she could and he fell on her as he pushed her out of the way to make it to his bed. She remembered her shoulder hurt so bad that she could barely write the next day in school.

Perfecting dinner time was a feat. Alyssa and her dad survived on mac n' cheese for a couple months, until Edmond decided to go grocery shopping and surprised his daughter with canned chow main, which Alyssa didn't like much. She adapted to the situation as best she could, learning how to take care of him, waiting and watching on the sidelines as alcoholism forced a warm embrace and wouldn't let go.

She entered back into the present, cowering beneath the blanket that her Aunt Danyelle had crocheted for her, the storm still carrying on outside. The blanket was filthy from overuse and filled with holes, but it had a certain power over the darkness that ensued, it protected Alyssa in some weird way. When she burrowed beneath it the scratching *sometimes* stopped.

Being a lonely little girl and roaming the streets on weekends, Alyssa got to hear a lot of strange stories. The place she heard tales of monsters and dark energy was at Adam's on the corner of Maple and Pine. It was an old run down building that used to be a repair shop but with a crap shoot economy it became a hangout for coffee drinkers and old timers. Mr. Wimbsley, and Mr. Adams, both in their late seventies, talked over many a card game and steaming cups of coffee, how they got up every day to join the living was always an amazing feat to someone of life and rejuvenation. They would always offer Alyssa candy sticks from a large jar that sat on top of an old tarnished copper register. Alyssa would take the candy and sit off in the corner playing with a favorite doll from a box of beat up toys. Even though the old timers didn't seem to care, they were watching out for her. They knew her story like they knew all stories that surfaced around town. It was their job.

They told many different tales that took Alyssa to very creepy places in her mind. She knew that it was the fault of those old men that woke a side to her that would have forever been closed if she wasn't there eating the candy sticks, candy didn't seem like a very fair payoff learning what she learned.

It was her mind, that corner of existence in the brain that the two old men shook awake.

"You remember, Johnny, from up the way, he took himself out to Sunflower Row, and took his own life." Mr. Wimbsley said. His mouth quivered after he spoke, signs of old age, and he reminded Alyssa of an old wise weathered owl sitting on a perch.

"Oh, yuh, the coroner said that it was suicide, but the teenagers, they're blaming it on something else." Mr. Adams would chime in. He was the listener through most of the conversations.

"It's a big secret out there, and no one knows what's causing it, but the storms, they tend to bring it out, or so it seems. The storm seems to sweep through, drop something with it, and BAM, death happens." Mr. Wimbsley slapped his hands together and Alyssa jumped

"There's nothing mysterious about it, we all go through some," the old man held his hand up to his lips to obscure them, but Alyssa heard what he was saying, *"shit."* Mr. Adams smirked and picked up a Swisher Sweet lighting it and puffing out gray smoke that drifted

into the air like something from the ethereal.

"Yes, living here isn't for this new generation, they can't take it."

"Well if you can't take the heat, stay out of Stevats, or whatever applys! I made a good life here, now retired here, and I turned out okay." Mr. Adams said and puffed again. He stood up and all his bones seem to rattle and crack like old tree limbs.

"Well, sweet princess," he said, standing up, *"It'll be dark soon, looks like you better get heading back home. Clouds are rolling in,"* he looked over to Mr. Wimbsley and winked, *"and you never know what the storm will roll in this time. Or the shades that stay behind for you."*

Both old men chuckled as Alyssa left.

Alyssa couldn't accept it, but had nothing else, so their stories and banter seemed tangible, something real to hang on to; she hugged it like an old friend. The horse blinders couldn't be lifted in the small town, the stereotypes couldn't be placed on back burners, and Alyssa, who possessed none of those, soaked in every ounce of lore, even if the stories and truth of it all was too scary to comprehend.

The shadow of those vivid stories, danced.

"You know it's all made up by those crazy kids, there's no other explanation..."

It danced in the shade of darkness when the sun set.

"When the storm rolls in, it really rolls in, and with it, who knows what will come? It brought it to only one kid when I was growing up..."

In the corners where peripheral vision served no more purpose and it danced in the moist dark basements under the old houses that lined the streets. But most of all those shadows formed monstrosities that waited.

"The kid, Tommy, disappeared, as an adult…but he came back to town, nothing kept him gone, no sir. Maybe there was good in that storm?"

Life would throw her tumultuousness, it would throw an unfair coin toss and Alyssa would eventually uncover what she had always wanted, in due time.

"He went away because he had a bad start, but changed for the better when he came back, remember he started that old general store in town, it thrived…"

The storm started to subside and sleep was heavy on her little eyelids. She cowered deeper into the blanket, into the warmth of security and eventually fell into the darkness beneath the bed, beneath the house and beneath the very existence she would have to endure for the rest of her childhood.

"Tommy was a survivor, that's what he was, not all people with an unfair start end up institutionalized."

As the rain and storm stopped outside, tears slipped from the corners of her eyes and she wanted to feel sorry for herself, but she knew it would just dump her into the same life of her father, and that, she knew, she could live without.

2

Derrick paced across the room looking for something to hit.

That *something* was Alyssa, thirty-five years old.

She lived in a world where she was immune to terror, fear and the unknown because it had overwhelmed her growing up. She was wringing her hands. Her eyes darted, looking for any heavy objects that Derrick could grab and whale her with. She knew that if she just handed something to him, he would belt her once and be done, but the living room was empty. If she didn't act quickly he'd pummel her over and over on her stomach and rib cage.

Derrick sold stuff on Craig's List, "Hot Damn! Alyssa, I just sold that sub-woofer from that old Jeep, remember it?"

Alyssa listened, and when it was safe to say something, responded, "How much did you get?"

"Enough! Okay? You're such a bitch. Shit, would ya look at this!" He stood up pointing to the laptop, "I just sold something else! I think were due for a vacation after all these sales, hell after vacation, maybe I can start a side business, ya know, start selling shit on the internet?"

Alyssa nodded, she was reading a book, disinterested and knew what could potentially come if she didn't at least confirm something, anything. "So, where we going?"

"Somewhere cool, somewhere we've never been, maybe Alabama." He said, pacing through the living room.

"That sounds fun, Derrick."

"You wouldn't know fun if it flew in through the window and hit your ugly face." Derrick laughed hideously and coughed. "Do we still have film for my camera, you know the one, it's the Canon that Grandpa left me in his will?"

"It's in the bedroom in the closet." Alyssa said. She got up and walked into the bedroom.

The closet door screeched open and she took the camera case down, making sure that it was in the case. She blew the dust off and took it out to the living room.

"Here it is." She handed the heavy vintage camera to Derrick who looked like a kid ready to eat something sweet.

"I can't believe it! I thought that old thing was thrown out, my grandpa used to say, it took great pictures."

Derrick snatched it from Alyssa and opened it, rifling around inside the case.

"Where's the fuckin' film!" His voice rattled the walls. "That's it, let's go, we need film for this fuckin' thing before we go."

The outdated camera was pristine and ready to shoot pictures. It had lived in a different world, a world that had been replaced by electronica.

"Derrick, do we need it right now?"

"Yes, we need it today; we're leaving tomorrow, dammit!"

Alyssa, who wasn't working, was apprehensive, but listened; she feared he'd pummel her to death if she didn't agree and this was the first time she heard about going on vacation.

His temper flared as they stormed the streets of Stevats and they couldn't find film anywhere. They drove all day looking for it and the revelation that the film didn't exist anymore burned the already short fuse Derrick had.

Derrick was a big man, his gut slightly hung over the belt line, his forehead was high and he'd probably be completely bald in the next ten years from stress and an inevitable heart attack that he would probably survive (the bastards of life usually do). He ignored the doctor's advice on losing weight because he rationalized he wasn't fat, just round in the mid-section. Sometimes, when Alyssa was drunk, which she only indulged in a few times a year, she'd ask him when his due date is? He'd only hit her in the arm for that kind of a comment; she'd slip it into conversation after he'd only had a few beers, with more than a few, he uncaged what Alyssa called the *"asshole drunk"* several drinks later.

There were levels of inebriation she'd categorized through the years, turning humor, into a kind of game. Alyssa was usually passive and accepted the abuse, and Derrick rode life's roller coaster of a consistent ride of indulgence in all that he liked.

"Take the camera anyway, Derrick, it's not the end of the world," she said, trying to calm the beast inside Derrick. She was hunkering in a corner of the couch, watching him get angrier by the moment.

"What the hell do you know?" His pace slowed. Beads of sweat ran down his red face.

"We're going to Alabama. Things are a little slower down there, maybe we'll find some at a store on the way down."

She half expected Derrick to charge her and hit, but instead he stopped pacing. She could almost see the light bulb click on over his head and imagined cogs of some imbecilic steel machine spinning slowly and awkwardly. He didn't charge her, or hit her. A large pearly smile filled his face.

"You're right, bitch." He did end up charging her but did a nose dive onto the couch and into her lap. This time, he took control.

Tonight, he was sober, and there was a ritual Derrick always performed.

He took a shower and walked through the house with just a white plastic apron around his neck. The apron was a butchers' or even a mortician's, it shrouded his large belly and only exposed his extremely hairy backside. He pointed to the shower and Alyssa had to take one.

After that he pointed to their bed. She would schlepp into it, and lay down. Her job was to act dead. Her pale skin, which usually never saw the sun, would be blindingly bright, in the dim room, and she was made to wear bright red lipstick that he'd hand her before laying down.

She lay stiff as a board, her arms to the side, her eyes closed, and she shivered. Derrick set the scene, metal table and autopsy tools, like he was working in a morgue. Alyssa played the part of a corpse. She hated it, and was thankful that it only happened once and awhile, having sex with him was creepy enough, the *"morgue"* ritual took it to the edge. Derrick got on top of her, breathed heavy and took control and did what he needed to do to fulfill his needs.

This was Alyssa's life, her dreams the only thing anchoring her.

*

Derrick was all smiles when the alarm clock bleated out a shrill beeping pitch at three a.m.

"Rise and shine, sweets!" He roared. The scent of sex still hung heavy in the bedroom.

Alyssa felt the hunk of meat roll on top of her. He kissed her neck and then jumped off the bed. She heard him shower and she threw some clothes on. She ventured to the pick-up truck and watched as Derrick compulsively checked each door to the house to make sure their fortress was locked. He jumped into the driver's seat.

"Isn't it too early?" She asked in the middle of a yawn.

"We're going to find film, isn't that what we talked about?"

"Derrick, we haven't even left Stevats yet, and you're bothering me about film. What's the matter with you?" She was groggy, and couldn't believe she spoke out of turn.

He slugged her arm, "You don't talk to me that way, I ask a question and I expect an answer, it's simple."

"Sorry. Can I go to sleep, it's early?"

"Why can't you stay awake? You do need beauty sleep, but it's annoying."

"Thanks, Derrick." Alyssa closed her eyes and propped her head on the window.

She dreamt little, but her dreams were vivid and made her feel like somebody important. Her dreams were a place that Derrick couldn't soil with the dark negativity that was such a big part of their marriage.

The man in her dreams treated her good, catered to her, watched her, and respected her. He would be her security. The dream shifted channels... she woke up groggily staring blankly at the repetitive scenery blurring past the truck...*security floated away.*

Alyssa was never important to anyone. She was a lonely little girl growing up with a father who only cared about booze. She remembered what her father said to her when she was a child, they weren't the nice things that father's said to daughters.

Her dad's voice haunted her as the past whispered ill-fated ramblings, *"Someday you should be so lucky to marry a man like me."*

That was her least favorite because she wound up with just that, a fat alcoholic who liked to dress up like a mortician and abuse her. Alyssa's father never abused the way Derrick abused. It was more mental from father, never instilling the things that daughter's need to hear to thrive and blossom.

"You'll never be important; you'll never be somebody, unless you marry a man just like me," the voice mockingly tittered waves of repetition inside her head.

She was haunted by her past; it crept up on her in her sleep like a ghost sneaking through the cobweb of consciousness. She stretched, yawning, coming to the surface of the here and now. She realized the truck had stopped and they were parked in a Starvin' Marvin's gas station. She saw Derrick inside flirting with a tall blonde. He poured two cups of coffee, paid for gas and grumbled to himself as he neared the truck.

"Got you something," he said getting in.

"Thanks, I could use a java."

"Here you go." Derrick tossed the cup at her and the hot liquid spilled over her legs.

Alyssa was wearing shorts and her legs were red

and pained from the spill. "Asshole!" she yelled.

She jumped out and doused her legs with the window cleaner next to the pump. She could hear his laughter. She took in a few deep breaths as her legs cooled. Fortunately, there weren't any blisters forming, only red splotches where the coffee landed.

"Come on, Alyssa, I was joking, get back in the truck, we have a few more hours to drive and we'll be there."

"Fine."

"I'll get you another coffee." Derrick ambled back into the gas station.

Alyssa was so angry she stared out the front windshield and hadn't realized that time lapsed, five minutes disappeared according to the green digits on the radio, and she didn't know where it went. Coming back to the crazy realm of Derrick she saw he was smiling and waving a package, jogging back to the truck.

"You were right."

"About what?"

"They had the film. This is fuckin' amazin'!" Derrick snatched the camera and loaded it. Alyssa heard the wheel inside turn and the automation of the camera came to life.

He pointed the camera at her, "Smile," he said.

"Don't waste the film, Derrick. Save the pictures for something better."

"You're right, you might break the camera." He laughed, it sounded adolescent.

"Can you drive?"

"You never want me to drive."

"I'm feeling artistic. I need to take some pictures."

"Okay. I'm just driving to the motel, right?"

"It's south of here, exit one hundred forty. The Rainbow Motel." Derrick said snapping a picture of the gas station's sign.

"I think I can handle it," she said.

Derrick snapped pictures like a little kid with a new toy on Christmas day, Alyssa felt good, for once in a very long time. She put the truck into gear, hoping that maybe things were getting brighter. Maybe this was the breaking point, she thought, the vacation might wake Derrick up and change him and end the abuse. Maybe the camera would help him.

She reached for her coffee and realized that Derrick never bought her one. She rolled down the window fresh air blew at her face, and she drove to the possibility of change.

3

They arrived at the Rainbow Motel, a colorful place, and that was the only positive thing that anyone could ever say about it. The wood siding was painted in red, orange, yellow, green, blue, indigo and violet, all rainbow colors from top to bottom and the roof was tiled with painted ceramic to match. There were beat up rocking chairs, also painted in the repetitive array of colors beneath the portico that covered a cement porch. Next to the rockers were rusted old coffee cans full of cigarette butts. The room numbers were tarnished copper nailed to the doors. There were several abandoned and stationary cars in the parking lot in front of some rooms that indicated full time residency. Small charcoal grills were set up next to air conditioners of each residence, yet the place seemed empty and void of people. Alyssa parked by the front office.

An Indian woman greeted them, a sign of life. Three small children were playing and watching re-runs of the Wiggles on television. A man, old and leathery, was climbing up a ladder and changing a light bulb in an outdoor ceiling fan that had wobbled to a stop.

"Can I help you?" The lady smiled, crookedly, a few teeth were missing and chipped, her English was broken. There was a pungent smell of body odor that wafted in the air when she moved her arms.

"We made reservations." Derrick said pulling out his wallet and handing the lady his driver's license.

"Okay, name please."

Derrick spoke slowly and Alyssa wandered around under the portico, room to room. She walked up to a door that used to have the number thirteen on it. The numbers were gone but there was a discolored mark that boldly highlighted what the room used to be numbered. The door was propped open and she heard a washer and dryer running. There were wood framed pictures next to the doors of the motel rooms. The wood was gold and carved in a fleur pattern. The painting was of a town nestled down in a valley. It reminded her of looking down at Stevats from atop Audubon Hill. There were tiny painted houses, lined up like pre-sixties style tract homes, over each house were blurry dark masses. The shadows were like little black storm clouds, each significantly different as if they were morphing into unique figures. Alyssa got a chill looking at the black masses, the dark grey clouds over the city in the painting, and the surreal obscurity of the scene which the artist was hiding. She turned away. As she walked in the direction of Derrick each room had the same picture and frame to the left of each door. She thought back to her childhood in the trailer park, under her bed, and wondered if the terror in the picture was what used to hide there. She turned away from the arcane pictures and thought about something as close to happy as she could, their wedding.

The furthest Derrick and she had ever been from home was Lake Unega fifteen minutes from Stevats when they camped at the rustic state park on the lake. It was for their honeymoon. They had an August wedding, the hottest part of summer, and Derrick was working part time as a janitor at Stev-Dev High School. They took the camping trip to celebrate and shed the dysfunction of a dry, outside wedding at the First United Baptist Church, complete with bees and a local band who only knew how to play Ronnie Milsap songs. It had been a memorable day.

It was in those woods of the campground that Derrick had shown Alyssa everything her naïve life learned when it came to intimacy. It was the consummation of their wedding day in a two-man tent propped on a rustic campsite. They had only camped for three days. Following the consummation, those three days were silent and meditative. They spent a lot of time wondering through the forest, swimming in the waters of Lake Unega and just enjoying what was before them. It was the calm that deluded what the future would hold, and if Alyssa had known at the time what she lived with now, she would have considered walking to the depths of the lake, not knowing how to swim, and let the dark nighttime waters consume her. Those paintings did something to her, *they* made her uncomfortable, and yet she knew that this was where she and Derrick needed to be. The pictures maybe just a sign post that created confirmation of this moment.

*

"Thank you, here's key, enjoy." Alyssa heard the Indian lady say. She was waving Derrick away.

"Do you know if there's a place to get film developed here in town?" Derrick asked before leaving the office.

"Quick Box, small place, it's at West Bench Plaza."

"That's great, thanks."

"Alyssa, over here," Derrick shouted.

"I'm coming." Alyssa trudged behind him into a musty room carrying two duffle bags from the back of the truck.

"The swimming pools in the back of the motel," Derrick plopped down on the bed, "and there's a place in town to develop the film."

"Can we just get settled in first?" Alyssa moaned.

"Leave it to you to put a damper on shit. I thought you *were* settled down, I did all the work to get us here."

"All the work?"

"The planning, the driving, the picture taking, and even registering us. Yes, all the work."

"Derrick, you're so…"

"What?"

"Never mind, let's just get our things unpacked."

The room was infested with black cockroaches that scattered when Derrick turned on the lights. Alyssa slid open the light blocking, stained curtains. The comforter, which Derrick plopped down on, was cigarette burned and stained with dry white crust; a few crinkled dead leaves rustled and blew into the air falling to the worn carpet. The drinking cups were hygienically-wrapped, but with long strands of black hair stuck to the plastic. It was cleaner than anyplace Derrick or Alyssa had ever lived. They ignored it, threw the duffle bags down on the bed, Alyssa glad that Derrick didn't go on a hitting rampage, and left for town.

4

The town was Americana. Empty, brick buildings lined Main Street and there was the plaza with Quick Box. It was run down and beat up; old stray metal shopping carts were strewn through the parking lot. In the center of this parking lot was the photo shop. There was a large haphazardly shaped, home-made, two-dimensional black camera mounted on top with "Quick Box" scrawled childishly in white letters. The sun was setting and dusk was bearing down, casting a golden hue as night tried to roll out. A large spotlight clicked on at the sign of dusk and lit the camera on top of the building.

"This takes me back a bit. We used to have a place like this in Stevats." Alyssa said. "It was by the old A&P downtown."

"Shut-up, Alyssa, no one asked you. I hope it's

open." Derrick snapped. He parked the truck next to the building and ran out, his camera in hand.

There was a door on the side of the building and in the front there was a window. Beneath the window was a drawer that slid out as if greeting Derrick.

Alyssa rolled the truck window down and listened as a mechanical voice spoke, "Please insert your film into the plastic container and place container in drawer." The voice came from a dull chrome speaker.

Derrick was reading a sign next to the window, a list of instructions, and his face scrunched-up, eyes squinted, he was clearly struggling to read it.

"Please insert your film into the plastic container and place container in drawer." The mechanized voice repeated.

The voice reminded Alyssa of a robot on an old series that was on television when she was a kid. Derrick didn't understand it or just ignored the fact that someone could be playing a prank on him. It dawned on her that some of the effects of alcoholism could really hinder one's precepts of their surroundings. All the demeaning, asshole things that Derrick ever did to her were now taking a bite back at him and his cool was heating up. What brain cells were left was like slow turning cogs trying to loosen and create his next movement or action, and the cogs were small fiery embers, steaming from red hot heat.

"Hold your ass, robot!" Derrick shouted and opened the camera to take the film out. He put the film into a small canister and set in in the drawer. The drawer shut, taking the film. "Wait a damn minute; I didn't fill out my name."

"Thank you for your business, please come back in an hour." The robot said.

"You don't know my name, God damn it." Derrick pounded the tinted glass.

"Please come back in an hour." Derrick slammed his fist against the glass again.

Red faced and sweating from the heat he stormed back to the truck and got in.

"Do you know what that damned thing did?"

"No. What?"

"It sucked my film off and didn't even take my name, like some sort of cheap ass whore. How the fuck is it going to know who or where I am in an hour?"

"It probably took your picture, you know, from that speaker you spoke into."

"Let me check this out." He stormed out of the truck and to the speaker. He ran his hands through his thick black hair and smoothed out small bristles of beard that was sprouting from a five o'clock shadow, as if posing for a camera "Is this thing on? Did it get my picture?"

"Please come back in an hour." The robot spoke.

"Shut-UP!" Derrick yelled and surrendered, he joined Alyssa in the truck, "Looks like we have an hour to kill, maybe we can get it on in the truck like old times."

Alyssa was at the point in her life that she didn't like him touching her at all. She knew if she said no, that he would be an asshole, if she said, yes, and submitted, a police officer would more than likely patrol the parking lot and bust them. She only hoped for an easy escape, but knew there was no escape, there was never an escape. She began taking her pants off. Derrick shifted in his seat.

Before he crawled on top, before he fondled Alyssa, dusk, turned dark, a very faint dimness hung over Quick Box. It was frightening, how suddenly the darkness came and how shadows were forming out of this dimness.

Maybe a ray of bright hope hides in the demure ensemble? Alyssa thought, thinking of the pictures that hung next to the rooms at the Rainbow.

Out of the speaker the robot voice spoke, "Your order is ready, Derrick."

Derrick's pants were half unzipped, and he hung, as if frozen, over Alyssa, his hand hovering over a breast. His jaw dropped, beads of sweat wavered above his eyebrows. "Did you hear that?"

"Hear what?"

"How the hell did that thing," he pointed at Quick Box, "know my name?"

"There's probably a person in there, Derrick, playing a trick on you."

"I'm going to find out." Derrick ran to the front of the window demanding, "Where's my pictures, you asshole?"

The black shade rolled up the front window, slowly, and a pimply faced teenager stared through the glass, "Hey, mister, you don't need to swear." He was petrified, his eyes wide behind the spectacles.

"Didn't you say my name a few seconds ago?"

"Yes, you took a picture of your driver's license. My job's boring. Don't blame me for shaking things up." The kid shakily pushed the drawer open.

"No." Derrick said. "You fuckin' freaked me out,

how much do I owe ya?"

"It'll be five sixty with tax."

"You don't know how close you came to me punching you through this glass, kid." Derrick said putting a ten in the drawer.

The kid slid a bright yellow envelope back out after collecting the money.

"That was fuckin' fast." Derrick said with a grin.

"Everything's digital now, even with the thirty-five millimeter, that's why we're Quick Box."

"Thanks," Derrick said, a little calmer, shifting his attention to the pictures bulging in the packet. He took the change and ran back to the truck waving the envelope like a little kid.

"That was quick! Let's look at 'em, babe."

"Can we wait until we get something to eat and get back to the hotel, Derrick?"

"Why do you have to fuckin' ruin everything for me?" He punched her arm.

"I thought we could look at them together back on the bed." She rubbed his leg and at the same time cringed inside as her stomach rumbled for food. She was starving.

For the first time in a very long time, Derrick listened to her, "You're right. You know I love to do it after our bellies are full."

He started the truck, popped a Ronnie Milsap cassette in and left the parking lot squealing the tires on the blacktop. The turmoil inside churned, Alyssa's heart leapt at every word that left Derrick's mouth, and his temper was erupting more quickly than it ever had. Alyssa worried for the first time in her entire life if that monster beneath her bed as a child was actually married to her and had somehow put on human skin to play dress up. She glanced in the mirror of the truck and the dimness over Quick Box became a dark forming shadow, like the paintings at the Rainbow, Derrick was driving too fast for her to see what it was forming.

5

It was a quickie, not in the truck or at the Rainbow, but eating lunch from a fast food joint. They didn't leave the truck. Derrick drove up to a microphone, ordered what *he* liked for both of them, and drove like mad back to the motel. In the room, which had a dissident mildew scent beneath the smell of fast food, Alyssa and Derrick sat on the bed and ate. Derrick shoveled greasy burgers, one after another into his mouth, washing it down with a swig of Coke. Alyssa slowly lost her appetite watching him, but was hungry, so she picked the pickle and tomato off her burgers and took small bites of the vegetation.

Derrick, through a gagging episode and a mouth full of food, spoke, "Man this sure is turnin' out to be a nice trip, isn't it babe?"

Alyssa was spent, tired, and not looking forward to Derrick pulling out a fifth of something and adding to his already spiked pop, let alone the dull dialogue. He would turn on the free porn channel, and slowly become the "asshole" drunk, so she didn't answer him.

"Why are you bein' such a cunt?"

"I'm not, Derrick, I thought the doctor said for you to stop drinking? And you've already started."

"I slipped it in some Coke while you were pissing." He said with a grin, "want some? My little friend Jack isn't gonna hurt me."

"I'll pass."

"The fuckin' doctors don't know what they're sayin', besides, my grandfather said that the fatter you are the healthier you are," Derrick patted his belly and fleshy waves rippled through the t-shirt he was wearing, "it takes me a hell of a long time to tie one on these days. So, it'll probably take a hell of a long time for it to catch up to my blood pressure."

"I worry about you, sometimes." Alyssa lied.

"I worry about me too." Derrick said, shoving the rest of a burger in his mouth and sucking down the last drops in the Hardees cup. He pulled out a fifth of Jack and poured. "Down the hatch," He sucked through a straw, "nothin' like catchin' a buzz quicker drinkin' it out of a straw."

Alyssa put the rest of her burger and cold onion rings into the bag and tossed it into a waste can next to the door. Numb wasn't a word, it was her universe. Never in her life had she grown so one dimensional. She used to care about people, about life, and now, she cared about staring out into space or someplace blank. She had given up, yet the energy inside her would not die, would not leave, and she was stuck with a fat husband who did nothing but add to her every day despair. Deep down there was a desire for an end, death, even deliverance. There was nothing in the cobwebs of her head that would sooth that deep pit of loneliness, because loneliness was another ingredient to the numbness that existed all along.

She remembered a time when she worked at Suncrest Nursing Home as an aide. She worked on the third floor; it was referred to as the "*Sunflower Wing*". It was the nicest decorated wing. Patients inflicted with long term or terminal ailments were put there, because they paid a higher price (make your contribution and you get a better seat). The wing was the prettiest and most elite.

There were stencils of sunflowers painted upwards on the walls and onto the tall ceilings; the blades of the fans were yellow petals of the sunflowers and the light in the center was the seeds. The greenery spread like an actual garden, all painted in three dimensional colors, shapes and tones, adding a bright ambience. There was a large aviary built on the south wall and when the sun streamed through the picture windows it refracted the colorful caged life of exotic birds.

The Sunflower Wing was a place the old people would be lifeless in bed or propped up in chairs drooling on their bibs. Their vocal chords unable to form words, their eyes milky as they stared off into space, colorless, and their mouths sometimes twitching as if they wanted to ask to leave the world, and could anyone help them? Alyssa wished at that time, that she could have granted them that wish, but she couldn't. She was like them in many ways, she cared for them and the life they still had, but knew they had grown numb to everything and everyone around them. In hindsight it was just a peak into the even bleaker future of her life, one she had no control of. Had she known then what she lived with now, the third floor picture window would have been a nice place to jump from and splatter to the plush green grass below.

She sighed at the memory, at her own oblivion of the contrasts, and at how even though she mentally disappeared, Derrick, was still in the room with her.

He stood up, his speech a little slurry, "I'm gonna watch some tv."

He flipped on an old tube television and turned the dial until it stopped at a man and woman, she in a nurse's uniform, legs up in the air and the man on top of her. Derrick muted the sound.

"Man, I wish you looked like that." He grunted.

"You could find someone like that, couldn't you?" Alyssa was walking a very fine line.

"Always a smart ass," Derrick said, he took another swig and set the drink down, "hey I almost forgot the pictures."

"Where are they?" Alyssa asked.

He poured another drink before answering, "I think I left them in the truck. Be a sweet-slut for me and get them, would ya?"

"Fuck you." Alyssa said. Her eyes darted to the ground in submission and she moved away from him, not quite knowing if she had made it out of the way of a beating or not, and if not, wishing that he would just beat her to death so she wouldn't have to endure it anymore. She needed a break, even if that break consisted of a two-minute jaunt out to the truck and back. Some fresh air outside would do her good.

Derrick laughed, which turned into a guffaw and tears slipped out of his eyes and down his red face. "I love you too."

When she'd already travelled from one form of abuse to another, concern, fear, even surprise were emotions taken out. Alyssa did what she was told and got the keys without getting hit. She hoped Derrick had forgotten how to be abusive and that maybe, counting her lucky stars that that part of his brain cells had been eaten away by the alcoholism.

The night outside was a black canvas, stars were like pin pricks peeking through the black, and a large full moon rose overhead, it smiled like an insane man. Crickets were singing in the woods and the sound of distant traffic was a low hum. Alyssa snatched the pictures from the front seat and just before she shut the door she saw something out the corner of her eye.

It was a shadow, not a shade of dark ink or paint forming above houses, like in the pictures, this shadow had substance and it tittered madly, it moved behind the trees just around the corner of the laundry room. She could make out the moonlight as it wrapped itself around the black mass, part of which stuck out from its hiding spot behind an old tree. Alyssa shivered, but stood frozen and scared. It brought her back to the moments in the trailer as a little girl. It took her back to the thunder, lightning and to the scratching beneath the floor of her bedroom that would stop as the boom of thunder or flash of lightning exposed the dark corners. The laughter, more like a tittering bird, or small child, gave her more chills, had stopped, and the shadow left.

When she thought she was clear of danger, out of nowhere, out of that corner that no one sees, the obscure places that hide things in the dark, a faint whisper taunted, *"I'm here, Alyssa."* She ran back to the room and shook the door knob, Derrick was laughing on the other side.

She tried to catch her breath, "There's something out here, Derrick."

He let her in and glanced outside, "There's nothin' out there, give me those pictures." Derrick's speech was slurred; he was on the brink of obliteration.

"Is that all you can think about, is your damn pictures!" She yelled.

"Sit here, slut," he said, patting the spot next to him.

Alyssa sat down as he peeled the package open. She tried to see the pictures as he flipped through them, but, he covered them with his hands, like an obnoxious child playing a game. His smile disappeared as he stared at one picture, his eyes not leaving it.

"What is it?" Alyssa asked.

"You're a slut, aren't you," His voice was still slurred but his face furled, his eyes triangles of rage, and his eyebrows creased, exposing wrinkles of time in those areas of the face not always shown unless the mask worn the most reared its ugly head.

"You've had too much to drink, give me those so I can put them away."

"Look, I'm not making it up, whore!" He demanded, throwing the pictures on Alyssa's lap.

The first picture was of his driver's license, he was holding it up, and she could see the dashboard of the truck behind it. The second picture was Alyssa sitting in the truck and next to her was a dark shadowy mass. It could have easily been interpreted as anything, like the game children play, looking up at the clouds and making creatures out of them. The shadow was nondescript, but had a humanly shape. The pictures grew more intense as the shade slowly morphed from picture to picture into a dark figure.

Shocked and terrified that Derrick was close to beating her again, she threw the pictures on the bed and stammered, "This must be bad film."

"I just purchased this shit!" He shouted. He was a good six inches from her face, Alyssa felt droplets of spittle hit her forehead, his hands balled into fists.

"Derrick, I don't even remember you taking these pictures. There was no one in the truck with me!"

"Who are you? Who are you?" He raised his right fist, put it down, raised his left, put it down and sat down on the bed, sobbing. "I knew it would happen. I knew it. I didn't think it would go this far, though."

It was uncanny enough to not feel her husband hit her, when clearly a moment of abuse had surfaced. He sat on the edge of the bed and cried. Empathy was something Derrick lacked. He didn't even cry or show remorse when his own mother died. Alyssa wanted to comfort him, but something inside told her not to fall for it, that it was an act.

Or wasn't it?

"Don't touch me." Derrick sobbed when she tried to put her arm around him.

"We can get through this Derrick."

"I knew it was gonna happen."

"What?"

"I heard about it as a kid."

"About what?"

"It was the Tulpa. It visited us all the time, usually

under the trailer we lived in. Those trailers were like tin cans, creepy as all hell when you heard somethin's claws scrappin' the floor joists."

He was talking about the same terrifying things Alyssa had experienced in her own life. She had never told him, or anyone else, about those events, and so she could not figure out how he could know, unless he really had been there himself. She listened because he wasn't beating her and for the first time in their marriage, they had common ground, a childhood terror.

"It visited us and spoke to us, Alyssa," Derrick sobbed louder, his chest heaving in and out.

"Derrick, talk about it, it's the only way to deal with it."

"Stevats had always been a weird place growin' up. There were rumors about ghosts on Audubon Hill, and there was all this talk that little kids could muster anythin', if they put their minds to it. We didn't believe it, at first, not until the shit started to come to life."

"What came to life?"

"We'd sit, my brothers and me, and talk about this monster. He was a tall man, shadowy and rough, he had claws on the ends of his hands and he lived in the dirt. Some of us called him the Bruised Man. We said that he would shrink at dusk and crawl through the dirt visiting all the kids in the trailer park by night to eat us and take us into the ground."

"Derrick, isn't that a kid's tale?" Alyssa was trying to convince herself more than anything.

"No, it was more than that. Half my friends that believed it into existence committed suicide in Audubon Hills, right off the cliff that the abandoned church sat on.

It was the Bruised Man; he had come to life by energy alone." He cried.

"Time to stop, you sound like a fool." Alyssa was scared. It was those damn old men who defined the energy of the town's conscious. They said it was like Big Foot and that if enough people believed in something it would morph into existence. But she and Derrick weren't in Stevats and if there were any rational thought on any of it the energy there would be there, not following people on vacation.

The energy would visit the salt mines deep in the woods, and there, in the dark shadow of the mines, the shades formed. A haunting voice echoed in Alyssa's head, and she shivered.

"I can't, Alyssa. There's somethin' else." Derrick hung his head. He was pathetic. His eyes sad and watery, his mouth in a frown, tears slipped down his face, and a sliver of drool hung down his chin.

"What can't you do?"

"I can't stop." He stood up, his face red again, his hands into fists and he punched Alyssa in the face knocking her off the bed and onto the floor. "A whore's, a whore's, a whore, and I married one. You saw the pictures, didn't you?!" He demanded.

She held her hand up to her nose to try and stop the blood, and held her head back. She could taste the iron as it poured into her throat and clotted in the back of it. There was a fine line in her, that short circuit in her brain that had kept rewiring, and repairing over the years, that repair stopped her from exploding and getting the best of the drunken asshole she called "husband." The maintenance wizard stopped her from killing herself, from slitting her wrists, plunging from the window of the Sunflower room. The signal, rather than attempt a form of caution, was telling her to kick his ass and she didn't know how to do it, or where to begin.

Derrick laughed. His laugh turned into a gut rolling hearty loud titter that repeated itself in a cycle of madness, a looping, broken record that shared resemblance with the laughter of her past. His thick black hair was disheveled and he kept running his fingers through it. He looked like a deranged clown without makeup, his shirt untucked and his belly plopped out the bottom and jiggled as he flared his arms in a bird-like gesture, each time slapping the tops of his legs.

"What are you gonna do now? Gonna call the Bruised Man in the pictures, is he your boyfriend? Where is he, Alyssa, outside, waitin' to ambush me?"

"I don't know what you're talking about!" Alyssa sobbed.

"I made that shit up. I heard enough of your whimperin' details in your sleep. It was a part of my bedtime story, those kids I grew up with, they were just fucked up, Alyssa, a made up creature didn't make 'em do it." He laughed uncontrollably.

"I believed you! For the first time in my life, I believed you were changing, Derrick! And look, you're still the fat fucking drunk that loves to control me!"

Alyssa had snapped, abuse or no abuse, it was the most lethal thing she had ever said or done her entire life. She stood up, trembling, praying that someone, even the monster that terrified her as a little girl, would come to her rescue, anything. She closed her eyes, things were hazy beneath the dark lids and she wept. Yet, if it didn't, death would great her none too soon, she hoped for either as she shook uncontrollably.

Derrick took out a hunting knife, "Open your eyes!"

Alyssa slowly opened them.

"I'm ready to use it on you, you've had enough beatin' for the night, and I need some lovin'. I'm done with talkin', I'm done feedin' your psychotic dreams. You're my wife and I do what I want to you, when I want to do it. Get your shower done! It's time to play! And if you don't play, Alyssa, you will pay; I will cut you up into tiny little pieces and feed you to the Bruised Man."

He pointed to the bathroom, his teeth shimmering from spit, and his smile a deranged smear of confidence, anger and total control. "You fuck with this man; you fuck with this knife!"

6

The mortician act was insidious.

Derrick's slithery, sticky tongue moved up and down Alyssa's skin and she cringed as each of his calloused fingertips touched her, rubbing her flesh and creating layers of goosebumps. She wanted to curl up and die, every writhing shift and movement from his weight was a crushing blow, and there was a possession that had taken out all of his drunkenness, replacing it with a rigid act of violence. He was forceful, stopped, applied more force until every limb, appendage, and mental state in Alyssa bruised, she was his to torment.

She forced a shut down, Derrick snapped his fingers and that sound triggered her awake like the snapping of an ammonia packet to a boxer's nose. There was white and then black, there was light and then dark as each time she faded into an oblivion only swam out of at his command, he *was* the master, he *was* the control.

"Wake-up, slut, you have a photo shoot to do and you're gonna play pretty for me."

"I don't..." Alyssa stammered. She stood, her arms folded over her breasts, exhaustion filling her entirely.

"That's tough shit. Sit, cross your legs, and smile with those pretty lips."

Derrick put the viewer of the thirty-five millimeter to his eye and snapped pictures. Alyssa shivered; the air conditioner shook the wall making her colder, as a continuation of the abuse played on. Her lipstick was smeared around her lips in a furl of red. Her pride was gone; any sense of anger, hatred, rebellion that ever tried to surface inside had fled like old dried snake skin.

All of her wishes of death as a means to escape this torment were null, she felt the dark warm breath of Death, could sense its dull throbbing existence nearby, and smell the dank dirt from whence it came. It smelled of rotten flesh and cavity, of blood, urine, and every biological element she imagined existed in the world. It was putrid, she held back vomit, it clumped in the back of her throat, as she endured Death's wide toothed grin.

She didn't want to die in an unfamiliar place where no one would come looking, no one would come asking questions. If she were to die, Derrick would go home and make something up, most would believe the story he hand-fed them, and all would eventually forget Alyssa was ever his wife. She had been one of those wives that hid in the marriage's background while hubby took care of things.

She worked part time in the beginning, at Suncrest, but slowly Derrick convinced her to get out of the work force, stay home, and maybe they could start a family. She counted her lucky stars that there were never children brought into this sick consummation. Tears slipped from her eyes as the weight of Derrick on top of her began, a repetitive motion. Through closed eyes and clenched teeth, the bedsprings sang as he finished another round and stood up, she could hear the camera being fondled.

She waited to die on the bed, lifeless and limp, unmoving and cold as a dank itchy blanket covered her legs. Cigarette burn holes in the blanket stared like eyes glaring up at her. She closed down waiting for the next time frame, the next movement, the next anything to confirm she could still breath, hear and could still cling to life. Derrick moved around the room snapping pictures from every angle. Finally, she heard the mechanized motor finish the film off and there was a wave of relief inside, maybe it was a window of reprieve.

"Get dressed," Derrick commanded. He popped the roll of film out and put it in the plastic container. His demeanor calmed, but his hands shook. He sat down on the edge of the bed and reached underneath pulling out his bottle of whiskey. "I need to calm my nerves, this damn shit don't last long enough." He unscrewed the top and swigged.

"I'm scared." Alyssa said, cowering naked in the corner. The dank carpet was rough under her feet. She sobbed uncontrollably.

"I've got film to develop. Get dressed." The wheels of madness had spun out of control, and there was no turning them back. "Fear, it's for pussies, like those idiots back home who hung from the oak up on Audubon, a bunch of pussies! And I didn't marry no pussy!"

*

The ride was tumultuous; the truck felt like it was on two wheels as Derrick took the curves of the roads too fast. The blurred forests surrounding them were a mesh of darkness and a distorted sound entered the open windows, Derrick seemed oblivious to it, but the sound, alien and dark, followed the truck. Alyssa sat, her hands clenching her knees tried to hold on to any rational thought that still remained. She heard the sound, it was distinct and tenacious.

She journeyed back to her past, she went back to a place when there was an ounce of realism, an ounce of hope, but still she was on the surface of consciousness enough to know the danger that was in the truck. She ambled across the proverbial, macabre, blistered tongue that served as a red carpet and tried not to stumble as she made way to that happy place.

"That's some strong candy, sweetie. I can smell it from over here." The old man said.

He was a gentle kind old man that reminded Alyssa of Yoda, with his wrinkled ancient skin and the wisdom when he spoke of a different time, and a different place. She was in the old garage watching the old men she had grown to love in her youth. It wasn't a great hang out, but it had always been safe for her. There was always a welcoming gesture from her elder guardians and it made her happy.

Alyssa smiled at him; it was a defense mechanism she had developed unconsciously as a child. She smiled at whomever and whatever people said to her, mostly it was a smile of nervousness and directed at those who never posed a threat.

"How's your daddy been?"

Alyssa shrugged; she really wasn't comfortable talking about her father, because she didn't know how he was. He was always slurring and stammering at the television. Filling her needs was the last of his priorities; she was smug in her thinking, simple in a complex methodology that was often the baggage carried around her entire childhood. Adults would never understand if she spoke anyway.

"Do you know the scratching under the floor?" The old man asked.

Alyssa stopped eating the candy stick. How did the old man know? How did he know that she heard the scratching and that she sometimes wished it would go away, everything would just go away? The old man looked at her, his eyes soft, his furled silver brows grandfatherly and gentle.

She nodded in confusion, but mostly because she wanted to hear confirmation that she hadn't made everything up in her head.

"It's your protector. Something that watches you, provides for you, and does whatever is in its powers to make you a survivor, Alyssa."

She listened in awe, in wonder as he was speaking. Never in her life had she anyone who cared about her and now she did.

"A lot of people my age, and hell, even younger, believe those mines were graves for all those Indians slaughtered by that mad man back in the turn of the century. Those weren't graves, those were spirit cells. The White Spirits, the Unega, they live in them, they haunt them, roam them, and they come back to us as shadow, to help those who need it. Innocent people, like you, Alyssa."

People loved something to fear and always blamed the native tribes of long ago for anything they couldn't explain. She had never heard it explained in a way that made her feel less afraid.

"It doesn't want to eat me?" She asked.

"No, have they ever done anything to you? They are watching over you, protecting you."

"They've never hurt me, just scare me."

"There will be a time, when the Unega come to help, sweetie, and there's nothing ever to be afraid of."

He took her hand in his, it was tough and leathery. Blue veins stuck out on the top of it showing age, it was freckled and swallowed her tiny fingers into it.

"How will I know when I need their help?"

"You will know because you'll feel more scared and terrified than you've ever felt. You will feel like you can't breathe, you will smell it in the air, like garbage, mixed with a lot of other bad things. You will know, without even knowing, and maybe even this little tête-à-tête will come back to remind you. You didn't have a fair start like everyone else; they will bring that fair start

back to you."

"What do you mean by fair start?"

"Your mom died, your dad prayed to the bottle, and you had to raise yourself. If I was younger, not so close to my own life's end, I would have swooped in and saved you. Unfortunately, my life is frayed, beyond mending, I'm at the end of my years, and will someday, hopefully, join them in the good fight."

Alyssa sat wide eyed.

"Now take another stick of candy and be on your way. Use those fears to generate a helping hand. Don't fear the unknown, embrace it and it will hug you back."

He let go of her hand, she left the garage with a fresh stick of candy, and she never saw him again, it was if he had vanished from her life, from the city of Stevats and from her world completely.

7

Alyssa woke with elation and Derrick shook her from the happy place.

"Wake the hell up!" He yelled, "We're here!"

Alyssa fluttered fully back to the surface; they were in the parking lot of Quick Box.

Darkness swallowed everything outside except the soft yellow glow from the lamp light, glimmering through the shadows, from the sign on top of the building. She wanted to believe in the fairy tale ending the old man had told her a long time ago, but the abuse took it out of her, yet it still hung tattered, a battle worn flag in her mind. All the fairy tales in the world had one thing in common, they didn't exist. Alyssa knew to make energy there must be the plus and the negative. She held on to both, a balance of evil, good, light, dark; her mind flickered, lost and dazed. She heard more commands from Derrick.

"Stay the fuck, here, you!" Derrick said through gritted teeth grabbing the film and slamming the truck door.

Quick Box looked empty, despite the twenty-four-hour promise, and Alyssa dreaded the outcome if they failed to service the psychopath who was the tour guide in his own deranged game. Derrick pounded on the glass. A window shade slowly rolled up and the once distant noise that pierced Alyssa's eardrums on the chaotic ride to the parking lot began its chorus.

The same nerdy young guy was there. *Didn't he ever sleep?* Alyssa thought. Derrick was screaming incoherently, from this distance, sounding to Alyssa like he was performing an old snake dance and speaking in tongues.

The knob to the door turned. The clerk stepped out and Derrick grabbed him. Alyssa tried to scream, a cry of worry and concern, of help, but the scream was caught inside her throat in a lump. The young guy didn't hesitate and ran toward Derrick. Alyssa was terrified that Derrick was going to kill him; she watched through partially closed eyes.

The man tried to tackle him, but Derrick was too strong. Derrick lifted him and with all of his force rammed the body into the side of the brick building. Blood began to spill out of his ears; the clerk's pearly whites were painted crimson with specks of blood. Derrick grabbed his head in one hand, as if he were lifting a basketball, and smashed it a dozen times into the stone.

"No one touches my WIFE, BUT ME!" He smashed the head into the stone again. The young man's face was turned into hamburger meat as Derrick swooped down to pick up the film and head to the truck.

"Can I help you, sir?" A robot's voice spoke from the speaker, and Derrick, sweating, his forehead wet and every strand of hair dripping, turned, slowly. It was as if time began crawling through mud, all sounds, all of time was ticking by, everything filmed lapsed and shown in some monotonous autonomy to Alyssa, the audience.

A ringing started; it was so loud that Alyssa stuck an index finger in each ear. She was trembling and couldn't control the shaking that took hold of her.

"You have film to be processed; can I give you a hand with that?"

The scene was ominous, the surroundings eerie. Adrenaline surged through Alyssa, fed by her fear, by her anger. The sky turned gray and dark, almost black, covering the early morning dawn, and above Quick Box, was a shadow morphing into something. It swirled like the eye of a hurricane over an ocean and in the center, the eye flickered, not by nature, it was something physical, something tangible, the dark mass was shaping itself.

From the center of the swirling eye, another formed, glowed bright bisque without a pupil, just two corneas, staring down over Quick Box, staring into Derrick. The arms pieced together a sinewy kind of cloudy mass, fingers outstretched with claws furling at the ends of the tips, but eventually, they became real life appendages not just gas and cloud.

The torso, dark and muscle with powerful threads of the storm cloud followed by two large stumps that reminded Alyssa of tree trunks from a large oak tree, attached were two feet, long sharpened toenails pointed like daggers. The monstrosity floated to the ground and then stood, towering at about seven feet, over its prey. Derrick, his mouth open, all of his teeth showing, glowing white through the gloomy darkness, his eyes were wide saucers as the glowing hypnotic stare of the demon beamed down upon him like some alien life form. The piercing tintinnabulation was coming from the creature's mouthless face.

Alyssa watched Derrick. He was speechless and for the first time in her life realized that her fear had dissipated, a small wave of security was saving her. She removed her fingers and the noise, once piercing her ear drums with pain, was a soothing melody. She noticed a large brown stain in the back of Derrick's Carhartt jeans, and a stream of urine pooled under his feet on the blacktop. His mouth hung open and drool ran down his chin, thickly and viscously. He was a lifeless dummy blankly staring at Death itself. He couldn't speak, he couldn't move, and fear had frozen him.

The shadow lifted Derrick. A small mousey squeak left the deranged, once powerful abuser. For a second, a brief moment in the history of the squeamish event, Alyssa heard nothing around her. There were no crickets chorusing in the dewy grass; there were no birds chirping in the trees. The sun and the moon were both battling for the dayside position, and all was as pristine as before a storm. Derrick's legs listlessly dangled in the air. He waved his arms around as life began to kick.

Alyssa grabbed the door handle of the truck.

She was about to run out to the thing.

To tell it to stop, as if helping a helpless animal out of a trap, assist the needy when frozen or frostbitten, but her hand froze and so did that thought.

The old timers used to say just before death, people see flashes of their life go by, flashes of memories, flavors, sights, or loved ones flit through your mind in a frenzied flicker. Those flickers, those peeks into the past are supposed to reassure the one dying that everything is going to be okay, that everything will subside.

As Alyssa's hand still frozen in fear, her memories eddying inside; they weren't of loved ones, of happy times, or anything that helps a dying person cross over. They were of every abusive word, every slap, every punch, and every demeaning thing she had endured in her short thirty-five years, and it infuriated her. The thirty-five millimeter was next to her on the seat. She noticed that Derrick had loaded it with film. She took the camera and got out of the truck.

The thing stood, holding Derrick in the air.

Alyssa's head still flashed through her past, her marriage, her shitty start as a kid and each event looped, over and over again. The Unega had come to rescue her. The gentle old man had been right. It fed off Alyssa's energy. Just as the last angry vision in her life zipped through her head, Derrick, helpless, dangling from above, in a whisper, faint and hoarse spoke, *"Help me..."*

After Derrick's last words, the thing shoved the upper two thirds of his body into a gaping hole where a mouth would have been. There were sharp pointy needles that began chewing. The bones and flesh ground together in a sick twisted crunch as the Unega's mouth masticated.

Alyssa heard the screams, the terror, and never in her nightmares had she heard as hellish a torment. She saw the legs kicking until they stopped. She put the thirty-five-millimeter camera to her eye and snapped a picture, and another, and another. Cold and emotionless, she snapped one last time before Derrick vanished completely into an oblivion. There was a flash of white light and Alyssa's vision went gray as she faded to black.

*

All nightmares come to an end, eventually. Alyssa knew that everyone would be missing Derrick when she went back to Stevats. And miss him they did. The Stevats' Chronicle interviewed her. She made up lies that everybody makes up when they've been through trauma and chaos, and they're backed in a corner. Hell, chaos had been her life for a very long time, putting words to it was not a chore and came easy. Attention eventually stopped, every last camera click finished and all print came to a screeching halt, because Derrick became old news. When the waters of her tumultuous tale had calmed she sold the house they once shared, and as soon as things cleared and the insurance company investigated the mishap allowing her to cash out a life insurance policy. She went back to work, gaining her independence, slowly.

In her new place she hung a picture, an eight by ten, above her door. It showed a clouded mass hovering over a familiar one-hour photo shop with the words "Quick Box" written in a childish scrawl on a plywood sign that had been shaped into a camera. The mass had no arms, it didn't have eyes or legs, or teeth, and when she looked at it her muscles in her arms and legs ached, as if she had run a marathon or lifted heavy weights the night before, and then it would pass. It was a brief synapse of energy that flitted through her, a nostalgic storm of the past.

Despite the discomfort of living that moment of reminiscence in the picture, it made her smile every time, and gave her hope day to day.

About the Author

Tim Eagle lives full time on the road with his wife, Maria and their dog, Cocoa. He grew up in Michigan and is inspired by the dysfunction, insanity and nepotism of small rural America.

timeagleportal.blogspot.com

Other Books
By Tim Eagle

Available at Amazon.com

Life Ship

Other Short Stories
By Tim Eagle

Also Available at Amazon.com

Symptom (Morpheus Tales #5 2009)

Vasectomus (writing as Jim Falcon) (The Gates of Chaos
Anthology 2021)